Drillmaster

Drillmaster

WILLIAM POMEROY

TNM Digital Media LLC • Chicago, Illinois

DEDICATION

Drillmaster is dedicated to the men and women who have served in the armed forces.

CONTENTS

ACKNOWLEDGMENTS

Thank you to Renee for digitizing this book and to my wife for putting up with me for over 40 years.

WILLIAM POMEROY

Chapter One

"What's your name?" cooed the Training Instructor, taking one quick step to face me squarely.

"Breckinridge, sergeant," I replied. Instantly the veil of anonymity, which was what made one invisible in the military, was lifted in a moment of impulsive undoing. Predicaments surrounded me like gnats in the summer heat.

I remember that day vividly, even though it was nearly 50 years ago. And then there were others later during boot camp I will never forget. It has amazed me the selective memory that conjures up what took place years ago, when I have a blank in remembering what I had for dinner yesterday. These events return with the sensual accoutrements of clear vision, palpable feeling, and distinct awareness. They are not a recollection, but an enduring memory that are in the deep recesses of the mind, stored there awaiting a trigger to surface. I can recall what I guess are turning points in my life, the quite often dramatic episodes that cause within moments billowy tears to stream. I believe these gut-wrenching emotional episodes are embedded in my soul, elements that chisel out my developing character, good or bad.

Just twenty hours earlier I had taken my first train ride, a continental country trip from Detroit to San Antonio, where I would get my basic training in the U.S. Air Force. I was eager to be taking it, leaving the blustery cold of the north for the warmer south, even though the weather had little to do with it.

It was an adventure beyond my own escapades, which got me into trouble regularly. I guess I was the typical middle child, trying to bring attention to myself through actions not with redeeming qualities, but I learned from them and that was enough for me. These adventures were mischievous, not malicious, although my older brother and younger sister occasionally found themselves in the crosshairs of some more dubious escapades. I knew the difference between right and wrong, but my sense of adventure overlooked the potential for someone's undoing. Too often this mischief got the attention of my parents, and soon ended up on my backside.

But learning was a vital element in any young boy. Did I know I was learning? Yes, because I felt better for it. Throwing rocks through glass windows of an abandoned two story dilapidated house around the corner from where I lived gave me confidence in my throwing capabilities. I had good hand-eye coordination which extended to an ability to wing the right sized rock into a targeted section of a broken window and winnow it down in successive throws that didn't entirely break it out of its fittings. What did I learn from this? Self-control when control counted.

Like in playing shuffleboard in my father's restaurant-bar on Tuesday night's Men's League. Put yourself in that atmosphere, under that pressure, you had better have self-control and good hand-eye coordination. The fact was, I was filling in for my older brother, who had been filling in for one of the men on my father's five-man team. Nevertheless, they expected a solid performance amidst the dense smoke and rallying cries of increasingly drunken men. I had to stand on a wooden milk crate to bring me up to the board's level. There I would receive the milk warm taunts of the other team while my father's team cheered me on as I sprinkled the board with sand, placed my hand on the edge of the board, eyed my target and pushed off the disc in a fluid motion. As it glided down the board, my heart raced with the need to belong, even for one evening, in a competitive atmosphere laden with acrid smoke and garrulous men heavy with lagers that spoiled their aim but held the attention of a young eight-year-old boy who reveled being in their midst, as I knew my father was. The aura of that evening stayed with me even as my brother replaced me the following week, amid roars that would crack the concentration of grown men, but not my brother. He was that steady.

The reason for my enlistment in the Air Force in the year 1960 was my failure to pass a college entrance exam at the city university. I was stunned to learn that I had not applied my high school learning sufficiently, although putting in the effort to make good grades in the classes I didn't like or couldn't understand easily, like higher math, didn't seem to matter at the time. I was found lacking to a small degree, but I was nevertheless embarrassed by this particular shortcoming. Little did I know then how often eye opening humiliation would cut me down to size in the months ahead.

My options were limited, according to my parents: getting a job or working for a living. It was their little joke. Instead, I took the inevitable other path, which was the beckoning finger of Uncle Sam. The draft hovered over all young males waiting for the most inopportune time to swoop into their lives and whisk them away to who knows where and for what purpose. I chose the Air Force because I had the idea in my head to do intelligence work during the Cold War instead of becoming a ground pounding warrior.

An Air Force recruiter came out to our neat little suburban Detroit home to explain what would happen to their son during his military experience. My parents were polite, that is, they didn't ask the question everyone knew was on their minds: Will their middle child, a second son, be whipped into shape and return to them a mature adult, like their oldest son, a task that they were unable to accomplish in their 17 years of dubious training?

The recruiter, who looked more the Marine type with a tight crewcut, taut abdomen and ramrod straight stature, was what my parents had in mind when I brought up the draft idea. He left leaving a clear cut impression in everyone's mind that I had made the correct choice of military units.

Once the die was cast, I found myself at the Fort Wayne enlistment center on W. Jefferson, a reddish orange brick monster that beckoned me with an invisible finger of welcome, unlike Uncle Sam. My first glimpse of what was ahead wasn't disarming. I was just one of dozens of new recruits who were being processed into the military life. The physical exam went well (having coughed properly) though the hurry up and wait pace didn't fit my restless nature. Their version of the entrance exam was hardly a choke hold. I turned over my test in such a short time that the Airman First Class, who was monitoring us, was perplexed. He encouraged me to check it over just to make sure I hadn't overlooked anything. I hadn't, so I rose to leave. Then I got my first "military eyeballing," that look that told me I was on the verge of making a mistake that I would pay for dearly. I was used to that look from my parents. I slumped back into my seat and waited until others finished. It was a long wait.

Quickly enough, I was restless and my mind began

to wander. It had me venturing into the whys of what immediately was going on around me. I admit to heavy thinking when I have the time to dawdle, though I admit I don't come up with answers quickly, just more problems to work out. Best that I could see from all that mental tasking was that there was this invisible team effort that was part of a new lifestyle. Acting separate from the others was a bad idea. That individualism bred thoughts of a singular nature. What I had to do, since I was a loner and was used to my own often quirky behavior, was to not bring attention to oneself, but hide in the masses, so to speak. To blend in anonymously and let things play out without my input. I decided on the spot to make a concerted effort to make a positive behavior adjustment.

After the first test was over for everyone, we were given a break before the second test was to be taken. I chose to walk around the historic fort, which rested on the banks of the Detroit River, upstream from Lake Erie. Although it was bitterly cold and a chilly north wind blew without respite, I felt the need to move apart from the others for a last personal outing before my new indoctrination of blending in took place. As I ambled toward the river, I could see Windsor, Canada on the opposite shore. Canada meant nothing to me, except for Canada Dry ginger ale, which separated it from the hometown Vernor's ginger ale, with a paler taste than the sweetness of Vernor's. Between the two I was satisfied with my selections of soda pop and wished right then for a Vernor's when someone called out for me.

"Hey, you there." It was one of the recruits, a short stubby guy who looked like a wannabe hoodlum. His stocky body came trundling down the slope, gliding through the thin necked trees like a skier, his hands grasping tree after tree and swinging himself forward like an ape. The similarity wasn't lost on me and I instinctively clenched my right hand.

"I seen you at the test," he articulated in a rush of guttural noise.

"No, I saw you at the test," I replied pedantically.

"I don't give a fuck about that stuff," he said brusquely, "but I can tell ya' you've got an ass kicking coming if you don't wise up." I seen how you acted up when that guy sat you down. Like you was better than us. You ain't.

"You aren't," I replied, again ever the verbal authority.

I didn't see it coming. He knocked me down with a single punch. An explosion of bright light and pain shot through me as I fell to the ground. My neural system tried to fix itself as bolts of light flashed and flickered in my head. Nausea set in and I rolled over on my back. I wanted to get up, but having lost my coordination, I foundered there trying to figure out when this short circuiting would end. Even as the pure blackness behind my eyelids slowly lightened, the pain persisted. I was a mess of hurt. Then the curtains opened. My eyes opened to a rush of maple leaves and branches. I moved my eyes perceptively and caught sight of a shoulder and then a face. And a big, smug smile.

"You get the picture now, punk," said Stubby, his eyes showing how pleased he was.

I laid back and closed my eyes, a sudden tiredness spreading over me. I don't know how long I recuperated in this prone position, but one thought kept sliding in and out of my scrambled mind: Why did I let him get so close? I apparently had other things on my mind, but nevertheless my fighting experience should have had the alarms going off in my head. I felt humiliated and angry for my stupidity. My vision cleared and I decided to get up. I did awkwardly, the effects of the punch not completely gone. I rested standing up, hugging a tree until everything around me was the same, except for the pain alongside my left eye. I lifted my hand to my face and felt for any swelling. I had been hit enough to know that blood would start to pool up there before long and start the healing process while leaving an oops.

I don't want to give you the wrong idea, that I was a punching bag. I was on the giving end of fisticuffs and was known even to make solid contact once in awhile, as my brother Walter could testify. After one memorable confrontation, he called me scrappy. I liked the sound of it but changed it from an adjective to a noun, Scrap. I reveled in that notion of not backing down when confronted. As I had just done. And failed miserably. Way to go, Scrap.

Suddenly it occurred to me that I would be late for my next test. As I entered the building, I was prepared for an audience of laughing and taunting faces. The hallway, however, was empty. I got to the classroom, but paused before rushing in. What would I say? Nothing came to mind except that I felt that I was in the wrong, that I got the due punishment, but how would I explain it with minimum ridicule. I could lie, say I bumped into a tree. Reluctantly I opened the door. Everyone was listening to the instructor. A sigh of relief spread through me as Stubby's pug-like face wasn't there. I quietly moved to a desk and sat. Unlike the previous test, this was harder and I was thankful for its length.

Once finished, I looked up to find someone staring at me. It was a slightly familiar face, but I couldn't place where or when it was known to me. He made a little wave with his left hand, like a smitten girl. I didn't know anyone who waved at you, much less in a room of guys. I didn't want anything to do with this guy, who did sort of look like someone I knew from eighth grade. Once my curiosity grabbed me, I had to figure it out despite his wimpy wave. Very little mulling over took place until recognition bloomed. It was little Harry Fowler. We had both delivered The Detroit News and had become fraternal friends even though we had nothing else in common. On dreary cold Sunday mornings waiting for the 4 a.m. news truck to drop off papers at the delivery manager's home brought every shivering youngster to the same level. A bond of sorts prevailed through our personal anguish. But that was light years away. We were no longer kids.

Chapter Two

Avoiding little Harry Fowler was impossible, although I tried. We had some similarities, the worst being middle kids. I recalled his sister, Tizzie, was the oldest by a couple years but didn't show it in the growth department. They were stick thin, with choppy red hair and voices that could stop a clock. They always complained about every little thing; incessant whining, like little goats bleating their displeasure that there was nothing to devour. Harry's younger brother and second sister were twins and, as I recall from Harry's whining, were plopped down on him while trying to watch television, like a bundle of laundry to be sorted out and put away. They were infants, called potato heads, which was Harry's way of saying Irish bred and born. I couldn't help but notice that Harry hadn't gotten rid of that noxious skin blight that seemed to spread like a virus over everyone in their teens, present company excluded since my mother tells me often that eating vegetables will cure anything. I knew it wasn't contagious, but it scared me nonetheless. That being the case it made me shallow to deny friendship to someone with bad acne. It saddens me to admit now that I own liver spots that have sprouted over my wrinkled skin and wonder if I will lose any of my few friends for that imperfection.

As my time for leaving home was fast approaching, I tried to connect with my parents a need for expressed love that unfortunately wasn't forthcoming. I never figured out that disconnect, although my mother's lineage was Italian, and that meant the first born male was special and treated as such, so that was a hint, but I ignored it, considering myself special, even if my parents didn't see it that way. Given all those spankings and Walter never even getting a stern look, it should have been an irreversible clue. My mother was the dominant parent, my father the go-along one, following orders passively while thinking he was the boss. So I guess I got my cluelessness from him.

When my father was not dispensing punishment to my backside as a young boy, he was working the New York Times crossword puzzle provided by the local daily I delivered. Crossword puzzle addiction was a stringent family tradition. His father could never be disturbed while working his, including sitting down at the dinner table when we visited, until he was finished. That irritated my mother, who believed that nothing interfered with dinner and didn't -- in her household. Take that, Dad.

Walter and I were addicted, too. Walter worked alone without a net, that is, without puzzle dictionaries, as did our father. When I was a novice in my father's eyes, he allowed me to assist him in his Sunday puzzle. Now, many years later, I still sought his approval via the puzzle. I approached him while he lounged in his favorite brown reclining chair, a clipboard in hand on which the puzzle was set. I peered from the side to see that he had just begun, only the top left quadrant was filled in.

"Well, you've finally gotten me out of your hair," I joked to my couch potato parent.

My father was an enigma to me. Actually all adults were a hard read, because even though I watched their lie detectors, I couldn't figure out what it was they were thinking. My father's lie detectors were a soft gray, like his mother's. I understood my grandmother and her eyes truly gave way to mirth and happiness when we visited, but occasionally she hinted, unknowingly, that something was awry, and I felt bad knowing that. I had recognized early that there were distinct differences in my second son father and his older brother, Henry, who was less like his father than my father was to his father. I hope I haven't confused you about this genealogy. As a youth I knew the differences between my older brother's personality and behavior and mine, but didn't understand why there were great differences, from attitude to overall behavior. We were from the same parents, so why weren't we the same. I know that sounds sophomoric, but I was sophomoric at that time. I know I have gotten off my point, so I'll return to the original non comment that started me down this rabbit trail.

Silence from my father.

"By this time next Sunday it'll be quiet as a tomb around here," I said.

He scowled, peering upward at me. I remained impassive. I learned from him about lie detectors, having started playing cards from the earliest cognitive year, which for me was about four. He told me the eyes showed "tells," that is, clues, of thought and action. Of course, he told my brother the same thing. Walter gave me so many false tells I stopped playing cards with him and was content to watch my parents, who weren't so devious.

He nodded to himself as he jotted down my four letter word for crypt, *tomb,* in the squares at 14 across. I continued to hover

"You're in my light," he said, flicking his hand at me like I was a mosquito.

Undaunted, I merely squatted by the side of the chair, eyes stuck on the puzzle.

He smiled, as I knew he would, resigning himself to my annoying presence. "Okay, for just four more, and of my choosing."

It was a game we played, but for me it was my only

emotional touchstone with him. And I accepted it. It had started out as one word, but slowly increased to five. One way or the other I would be able to solve five pieces of the puzzle, after which I could no longer hover or bother him.

He pointed to 32 across. A seven letter word for "common." Quickly I responded "*ignoble*" in an insulted manner as if to say you've got to try harder than that.

He moved on, entering the important fillers that I had difficulty with, like New Guinea town (lae) and genus of olives (olea). His memory was voluminous and more to the point, he never allowed a crossword dictionary in the house. Quietly I watched as his No. 2 pencil steadily filled in blank after blank. He hesitated, giving me hope. Aha. It was a five letter word for éclat at 42 down. If I didn't know it outright, I had a minute to figure it out. The answer eluded me, so I started sorting out possibilities in the words around it to pick up a letter or more. His pencil began tapping on 42 down in a resonant countdown. He knew it unnerved me. And it did. My mind quickened its pace of sorting out letters. On the verge of giving up, it popped into my head. "*Glory.*"

He shook his head in mild disgust instead of saying lucky guess.

I don't know how you'll be able to finish the puzzle without me helping you, I said, smiling.

"I'll figure it out," he said drily.

A week later I walked out of their lives for four years, except for occasional letters from me. There was no reciprocity, which did not puzzle me in the least.

Once on board the train bound for Lackland Air Base in San Antonio, Texas, my next encounter with Harry took place, and it was more to my liking because it included a money game of cards taking place forward in the dining car. I moved gingerly through the trundling train amid flickering lights from a city's neon wardrobe, my legs not yet used to the bump and sway of the train. I felt a deep sense of relief now that I was on my own.

Little Harry was standing in the aisle peering at the cards of a black guy among three others who were playing cutthroat pinochle on a low table they had appropriated from somewhere. As I approached, I saw Stubby in the game, quite intent as he studied his cards up close to his face, his eyes crossing. I tried to be inconspicuously silent. Soon a miscue defeated the bidder and jeers thrashed him.

"Gotcha, big time," exalted a well-built Negro, pushing himself away from the table with one hand while the other was thrust at the loser in a belittling manner.

Little Harry looked up and saw me. "Hey, Jonnie," he blurted, overjoyed to see me.

"Harry," I said, less than enthused with his giddiness than the game itself.

"Hey, guys, this is Jonnie. We were paper boys together," he exclaimed too loudly to the others. The black guy eyed me in the same contemptuous way he ignored Little Harry. Then Stubby looked my way.

"We've met." He made eye contact and smirked. "Come on, deal."

I felt some relief that he didn't say anything, but that was quickly set aside when my natural instincts kicked in. I had to get in the game. I peered at the scorecard to see that one player was far ahead of the others. I looked at each player to figure out who had the lead. Harry was talking in my ear while I looked for some sign. The black guy got my vote. His dark eyes revealed nothing. He had the quietly confident look of the hustler.

On the next deal, he passed with the best hand, which I saw as I feigned interest in what Harry was saying to me. Required to play the hand if no one bid, the dealer made his forced declaration. The black guy melded nine with kings and a trump nine and coupled with big cards, the dealer was easily set. No one challenged his sandbagging. The big loser squirmed in his seat as he doled out his losses.

"Anyone leaving," I inquired.

"Yeh. Can't catch a cold," said the loser. "Let me

out a here," he said, getting up.

Stubby got up to let the loser out and turned into me, a big grin flashing. "This'll be interesting."

The game was a hundred points, at three cents a point. Winner got paid by all and the others paid the differences between them.

In roughly two hours, I'd won $9.41. The black guy, listed on the scorecard as Tell, mentioned a change to euchre. We drew for partners at a dollar a game, fifty cents for every set. I ended up with Tell. We played through St. Louis and I saw the Golden Arch lit up at night. Tell and I won $22 each and I had secured rights as Stubby's Enemy No. 1.

When I woke up, it was early morning. I had no clue where we were.

"Where are we?" I asked.

"Okie-homa," replied Tell in a flat, tired voice.

My back was a bit sore because of the awkward angle I had slept in. The guy next to me in coach abutted me on the butt, but my butt was warm. I had to be warm to sleep so I fashioned myself a cocoon to sleep within. Whatever I have to cover myself, I cover my upper body, including my head, except for a peephole. My father called me "The Monk" because of the cowl I created. My sister extended that into the Monkey. It was her little joke.

I picked up on that flippant tone, and curled out of my cocoon. The sun slashed across my eyes, blotting them. I twisted away and sat up, while rubbing my eyes.

"Don't wear them out, kid," said Tell's voice.

I shuddered off the erratic sleepiness that comes with lengthy traveling. Wake up, brain. I stretched and opened my eyes. Tell sat across from me.

The country had a rural quietness that reminded me of Indianapolis. All I had ever heard of Texas was that it was an extension of Mexico. This couldn't be Texas. The rolling hills and naked trees nestled around farm houses looked like the Midwest I grew up in. The skies were dreary and the wind whipped and bent trees. At least there wasn't any snow. This, however, wasn't a reprieve. It looked desolate and unwanted, and I began to wonder if I had blundered with this military enlistment thing. But I had no idea what any state looked like, except suburban Detroit and rural Indianapolis. But those divergent scenes gave me the impression I knew that was what most of the country was like, except for the mountainous regions, which I knew from movies.

"What time is it?" I asked.

"Doesn't matter," Tell replied.

"Why not?"

"You ain't going anywhere but where the train going. Don't think about time. Just relax and enjoy the ride," he said flatly, a tone I had gotten familiar with since we met.

For reasons unknown, I didn't trust Tell. There was something about him not understood. He seemed totally detached from anything around him. Like a professional something. His eyes blocked out from any emotion, even as he joked. He seemed to be playing with us.

"Are you a hustler?" I asked directly, my voice rising a bit in anticipation of his answer.

He smiled, showing ivory in a background of ebony. "Why you say that?"

"I think about last night and I get giddy. I got twenty two dollars more in my pocket and happy as a flea on a dog. You, on the other hand, are unfazed, not even playing at being thrilled.

"I don't thrill."

"I guess it doesn't matter anyway. I'm not planning on gambling any more, especially not against you."

'But, you will." Then he smiled, in what seemed genuine, but his eyes stayed dark.

"Think so?" Why is that?"

"You like the action and I brings it. You are

watchful, but you can only read so much. You think you can read me, but there's no tell about me?" Again the vacant smile.

I didn't mind parrying with him. I was too curious to let it go and I was sure he knew that.

"Is Tell your real name?"

"Does it matter?"

I was not that good in the endgame. I knew openings and could handle the mid-game, but I was weak here in the trade game. My curiosity dissolved into a mild satisfaction. I had to be patient and alert. Soon another thought occurred.

"Are you on this train for the same destination as we are?"

"Remains to be seen."

I got a glimpse of something irregular in his face, but didn't know how to process it. My best I guess was that he got aboard through someone he knew and abetted him in order to separate us from our cash. It was a good M.O and easy pickings.

The train made a stop in Fort Worth. It didn't look like a fort, but I considered it was when the Indians were on the warpath. It was a cattle town, I knew, from Louis Lamour novels. It was still a cattle town, and we were the cattle, being shipped southward to San Antonio instead of the reverse.

I went up to the dining car. Instead of the boys of last night, the car was filled with ordinary folks, a couple of pretty girls included. The one that caught my attention was a redhead, a perky lass from her animated conversation as she pointed out the opposite window to the train yard. She sat with maybe Mom and probably sis, although sis looked a bit frazzled and, worn out. I had no idea what Texas women or girls looked like, but this wasn't encouraging. I expected cowgirl hats and boots and a lot of razzle-dazzle or maybe hoped for that look. Mom and sis looked like farm people, ordinary and tired looking. But not the redhead. She was very pretty, but looked hell bent and prepared for a mix up. She was feisty alright, as I quickly found out.

"Is this seat taken?" I questioned her as I walked up to the empty seat next to her.

"Looks empty to me, don't it."

"So I can sit there?"

"You must be with them other boys," she said with the emphasis on "boys."

"Probably."

"Don't you know?"

"If you mean the other recruits, yes, I guess I am."

"Plunk her down then."

"I'm sorry, what?"

"The seat is available. You don't get around much, do you?"

I sat, looking at maybe Mom and probably sis, who stared intently on me as if I had just farted. I felt an embarrassment creeping up on me. I was clearly not welcome.

"That flustered look y'all got is sorta cute," said Red.

"I'm new. I mean, everything's new to me."

"Still a babe, you are. But that's just fine with me. Maybe you can teach me something I don't know."

"That'll be the day," said probably sis.

Red arched an eye toward her.

I couldn't help but stare at Red, who was the next level up from just pretty. Pretty didn't quite get there. Beautiful was a stretch. The in between was very appealing, as was the blouse. Not exactly the blouse, but the opening that showed a portion of her breast. I admit interest in the physics involved. Back in high school girls were all sizes: small, medium and large in the apparent breast size. I was sure I could tell pretty well who belonged to what size until the post graduation pool party. All the girls had revealing swim suits on, and I was flabbergasted. How could so much breast look so little in a bra.

"There's nothing wrong with your eyes, is there?"

"What? I'm sorry. I was distracted."

"Probably thinking of something you'd rather not let me in on?"

Getting caught looking at a girl's boobs was natural and embarrassment played no role, but Red came to the point, which was where embarrassment lived.

"Like what you see?"

Yes, "I was looking at your breasts … and." I hesitated to see how she was taking this and decided that I should finish, staying the gutsy course so not to appear weak when challenged. I had decided on 34s.

Without missing a beat, she said, "Have you figured out the color of the nipple?"

Who talked this way? Maybe Mom had turned away disgustedly, but probably sis was amused.

"Pink, probably, 'cause of your hair being red."

"Naturally."

I was mesmerized by her attitude and evidently curious "My name's Jon, if you're still interested."

"You've got my attention Jon, so you might as well make the best of it."

Her light brown eyes sparkled and a small creeping smile started to form. I waited for a full smile, which I wanted as a declaration that I was fully welcome. Instead she paused and then introduced herself.

"Rose McGaffey's my name, and yes I am still interested. You going to Lackland?"

We talked in an unrestrained manner, like friends who had not seen each other for awhile. She was a first-year student in a place called College Station and was thinking of majoring in psychology. Later on she gave me her address and asked that I write her and maybe after basic training to come see her. I was on the verge of falling in love when we were interrupted by Stubby and some others I had seen him with during the trip. They looked rough and ready, which made me wonder why they hadn't enlisted in the Marines or one of those special forces in the Army.

"Whataya talking to this loser fer?" Stubby said, chuckling.

Before I could reply, Rose laid her arm on my arm. I hesitated long enough for Stubby to titter and Rose to take dead aim on him.

"Didn't seem that way to me in that card game earlier. All I heard you do was whine." Rose's voice had turned hard and suddenly I became uncomfortable. I knew I had to do something, but couldn't think of what as Stubby and Rose stared at each other. Stubby wasn't fazed by her rejoiner. He tittered again, staring right back at her. They eyed each other as I became more uncomfortable. I was ready to trade punches rather than hear her hard voice again. But she beat me to the punch.

"You can go now," she said to Stubby. There was no questioning her tone of dismissal.

"Wasn't interested in you anyhow. Just come by to tell the punk here to watch his step. You got that punk?"

His malice, I admit, worried me and I think it showed, because he tittered again, turned and walked off.

I half turned to Rose, who was looking at Stubby swagger away. Then she turned to me and smiled but it was a crooked smile and I felt that I had somehow disappointed her. Nevertheless she wrote out her address and smiled in her pretty way when she offered it to me. That momentary disappointment vanished but the invisible remnants lingered imperceptibly and again I didn't know what to do about it.

We talked a bit more but there were more silences. In a way I was relieved when her stop was announced. In departing, her warm hand brushed my hair and she gave me a warm smile. She said nothing and I took her cue and remained silent. And then she was gone. I held the piece of paper with her address in my numbed hand for a long time, wondered when exactly I would toss it away. I felt defeated and passed by.

Way to go, Jon.

As the train clacked along, I sat away from the others, who decided one last round of whiskey was necessary. It wasn't my duty to remind them that they were in the military and getting off the train in a drunken stupor wasn't the way to start off boot camp. I planned to follow orders and keep quiet until I got my footings.

The weather wasn't what I expected. When the train pulled into the San Antonio rail station, I could see heavy coats worn by railroad personnel and their cold breaths. I'd worn what the recruiters suggested we wear: layers of light clothing, which could be mailed back home with our first letters from boot camp. I pulled out a light blue sweater from my travel bag and the remainder of a bag of white grapes. I ate the grapes while pulling on the sweater. My favorite jacket followed. I looked out on the platform to see two noncoms, dressed in winter blues and smoking cigarettes. I knew a bus ride would take us to the base, but neither looked like busmen. They looked anxious and I picked up some movement that I easily recognized. They were bouncing slowly on the balls of their feet, to keep the blood flowing and help warm their bodies. I had learned to do that on cold wintry mornings waiting for newspapers to be delivered to the station manager's home.

That single thought stuck in my mind as I added clothing to warm myself. I could envision myself alongside them, shivering, bouncing slowly on the balls of our feet and joking how fucking cold it was. Knowing how it felt, it changed the way I looked upon them. And I wondered if that was a lesson learned.

Chapter Three

The buses that collected us were Air Force blue. We piled into one as a thin black man with two stripes standing next to the doorway told us to keep moving. I found myself a seat up front, sensing from my country school bus trips that the back of the bus was where trouble began. Not surprisingly Stubby swaggered to the very back. Little Harry found me with little difficulty and slid beside me.

"Ain't this exciting," he blurted, a little too loud I thought as the snickers came from Stubby and some cronies he assembled.

"Oh, I am so excited," came a reply in falsetto from somewhere in the back, and then laughter that seemed to stretch out forever. As much as I wanted to get away from Little Harry, I felt I had to stay with him for his own protection. Stubby and his boys were getting rowdy as we sat waiting for the bus driver to get aboard and get us moving.

I had already swept the bus looking for Tell, to no

avail.

Seconds later, the two striper eased up and stood beside his seat rather than sit. He stood there, his eyes searching us. Then quietly, but intently he strutted to the back of the bus. The noise had not abated, as if his presence was no threat to anyone. He stopped, looked directly at Stubby and shouted: "Quiet."

Titters met his declaration.

"You. You." he said, his hand indicating to two Stubbyites.

"Out! Now!' Reluctantly they eased out of their seats. The two striper moved aside in the aisle and shouted: "Move."

They scurried out, followed by the two striper. I didn't hear what he yelled, but when I looked out the window, I saw them both on the ground doing pushups in front of the bus. Both struggled to do them precisely as ordered.

"More," he yelled. "You, get your butt down."

Absently, I looked back to the back of our bus as another Stubbyite asked what was going on. Someone yelled "pushups. He got 'em doing pushups."

"Fucking nigger," came a whispered reply.

Using the "n" word, in the presence of other

colored on the bus now would be like lighting a powder keg. I looked at one beefy black man, who turned around in his seat and looked hard at Stubby. I expected him to rise and confront Stubby, but he didn't.

"Cracker," he blurted, stone-faced.

"Spade," Stubby said.

And then a rejoiner: "Honky."

Someone tittered, and then came up with "spick."

The beefy black man said that was a beaner name, and laughed, shaking his head in disbelief. "Boy, you gotta get your peoples straight."

I wasn't sure which way this was going to go, but I was uneasy. Then another euphemism was thrown out and more laughter followed. My anxiety waned. Somehow the tension disappeared in a silly word game that stretched to inanity. I offered "hayseed" but by that time everyone had settled down and no one responded. The stillness was a relief and the quiet stretched out harmlessly.

"They're coming back in," someone yelled from the front row of the bus. Sheepishly both of the boys went to the back of the bus, one's red flushed face a sign of his punishment. Our stillness was pervasive. Not a peep nor titter.

The two striper stared at us a couple of seconds then

turned and sat in the driver's seat. We pulled out moments later and I felt some elation that I was on to my newest adventure.

I had a pretty good idea what to expect at Lackland from photos at the recruiter's office. At the entrance to the training air base, a uniformed airman second class with a white AP band on his arm waved us onto the base. Once inside I felt my adventure finally taking hold of me as a marching flight came to a crisp stop at a stop sign just outside my window facing me. The way they came to a crisp stop, without any wavering of bodies, caught my attention. Even though they were dressed in green fatigues, their shiny black boots gave them the look of an elite group, even though I could see they were slick sleeved and being led by a young airman third class who was positioned half way back from the front. He looked terribly young, like myself. And I could see me doing just what he was doing, exacting timed movements from his charges while brimming with confidence. As the bus moved on, I could see two airmen leave the phalanx and go into the street with hands raised to stop traffic. I twisted upwards to see exactly what they were doing when the bus driver yelled at me to sit down. I reluctantly obeyed his command.

A Stubbyite chided me. "Bad boy, bad boy."

Without thinking I gave him a digital reminder of what I thought of him, which brought a chorus of "ooos" and a snappy "Be quiet back there" from the two striper.

Under cloudy skies, the bus continued on to the base processing headquarters.

When we unloaded in a large parking lot, other buses were unloading their recruits. There were hundreds of us, many bundled up but some only in brightly colored shirts. I guessed correctly that they were from California or Arizona, and probably didn't own a winter coat. Some of the Stubbyites howled over their light wear, labeling them stupid surfers.

Then the two striper called out our names and separated us into six different groups. He pointed to designated areas on the where each group was supposed to meet up with others in the same flight number. My group number was 1416. I saw a placard with 1416 and waved our group that way. Harry was in 1416, as was, as luck would have it, Stubby himself. Our group was just six. When we reached the 1416 group, many of the bright shirts were there, too. The only exceptions were the absence of any Negroes. I had hoped Tell would end up in our flight. I felt the need of a friend besides Little Harry. So there we stood, a motley group, thrown together from heaven knows what part of the country, as different as different could be, or so it seemed.

"What's going on?" a long dark haired bright shirt asked me. Everyone was just standing around waiting for some information on what was going to happen next. I felt pleased someone would ask me, even though I was clueless.

"From what I'm told, we're here to be picked up. Aren't you cold?" The temperature had to be in the low 30s with a blustery northern wind tightening our skin.

"Naw," he said as if bored with my naivete. "As long as I know there's a warm spot ahead, I'm okay with it."

"I know what you mean," I said, smiling knowingly, but more because we had something in common.

His dark brown eyes turned to me, as if it was okay to say more. So I did. "I used to freeze my ass off on Sunday mornings hauling heavy Sunday papers on my paper route. I made it only because I knew I had a big cup of hot chocolate waiting for me at home.

His darkly handsome face nodded. For reasons I would not be willing to express to others because of my naivete, I thought of him as Hollywood handsome. He would be attractive to the opposite sex with his facial features, particularly the dark brown eyes, I guessed, because they seemed to sparkle at times, along with a remarkable smile and white teeth. And he was acne free. His lanterned lower jaw and contagious smile reminded me of teenage heart throb Ricky Nelson, whose quick wit made him an endearing character on the family television show featuring his parents Ozzie and Harriet Nelson. It was my favorite TV series and was even watched by my parents, who suggested that my wisecracking was not unlike Ricky's. The comparisons ended there for them, although they resurfaced years later when I met and fell in love with my wife. Because of our similarities, I thought we might end up in a friendly relationship. Taking that to heart I decided to introduce myself, and did, and even extended my hand.

His response was a faint smile and internal workings that had me wondering if I was being too forward. Then his hand came up.

"Estaban Leeds," he said. And we shook hands, his grip much stronger than mine.

I was perplexed by his mixed ethnicity, and rather than think about it to myself, I must have shown a tell.

His eyes shifted disconcertedly.

Hoping to avert a misunderstanding, I blurted, "What are you?"

He studied me, his eyes sort of rolling about slowly, like eyeing me as a fetching girl. Then he gave out a faint smile. "Human being, you moron."

I laughed, enjoying his quickness and impertinence and the fact that I was a moron at times, like now, when I let my curiosity run rampant without my brain having any input.

Estaban reached out and patted my shoulder, a

broad smile spanning his face, and he spoke: "Say, is there any chance I could borrow your coat. I'm freezing my ass off."

"Well, I don't know. Maybe there's a moron around who could . . .

"Who you calling a moron?" said a voice off to the side.

I turned to a skinny kid with a heavy Duck Ass black mop of hair and a face of acne."

"That ain't a way of being nice," said Little Harry, coming to my defense.

DA Hair repeated Little Harry's comment in a snide way, during which I figured out he was from the East, and probably New York. Everyone knew all the wise guys lived in New York. Little Harry was pissed and since they were about the same size, Little Harry might take him on. Little Harry and DA Hair stared at each other, both showing contempt for each other.

Ain't cold fer us," a tall, lanky bright shirter said looking at the two roosters posing. "Water's colder. In the morning sometimes we have to wear wet suits it's so cold. But Jake's right, this ain't cold.

I nodded, awaiting the outcome of the rooster pose, when someone grabbed my arm. I turned to a hairy, burly guy who had bad body odor.

"You know where I can take a piss around here? I really gotta go."

Mr. Information was plumb out of answers. I don't know whose facial expression was dumber, but I believe it was his. As I struggled to respond, Stubby rose to the occasion.

"Why don't ya piss in their direction," he said pointing to the Bright Shirts, "they can surf on it."

Fuck yous came in unison and I thought the roosters weren't in the same league as what these West Coasters had in mind for Stubby. More posturing took place and something was on the verge of happening. Who was on whose side hadn't been determined, but I didn't want anything to do with it. Some of these boys were big. I wished I had a loud authoritative voice to stop this, but I would be lucky to muster up some spit.

"Boys," boomed a loud authoritative voice, followed by the presence of a tall rawboned man who inserted himself in the middle of this pending brouhaha. A red shock of hair sprung out of a face of contorted angles. It was Daniel Boone himself, with a big Adam's apple the size of a big acorn.

"Those of us yonder don't want a fight with you boys cause we ain't et yet and are tired from the travel, but if you're so inclined, we'll take you all on."

"You're a big 'un," said a lanky Bright Shirter, who

seemed small compared to Daniel.

"And mean when I get my dander up, so you best know it now," said Boone.

No one doubted the outcome should someone drop a hat and all hell break loose. Everyone returned to what they were doing, quietly muttering about when we were going to be collected.

I introduced Estaban to Little Harry and told him how Harry and I became friendly. "I just remembered that fight you had with that Slocum kid, over an ice cream bar."

"Yeah, he knocked it out of my hand and kept going without saying a thing," said Little Harry, quickly responding to the attention drawn to him

"So you jumped him and pushed the dirtied ice cream in his face."

"He had it coming. He could have said it was an accident and apologized but he wasn't that kind. So I jumped him."

I turned to Estaban. "That was the best fight we had that whole year." Just that quick another side of Little Harry I'd forgotten about surfaced and I had to rethink who he was.

"Nope. Jefferson's was," Little Harry blurted, now on a roll.

"Missed that one.

"You scuffled with Big Manny, didn't you, and broke his nose?"

" 'Til he threw me on the floor and jumped on me. He knocked the wind outa me, but his punches didn't matter cause I couldn't breathe."

"We dragged him off ya. 'Member?"

"I think I passed out. Remember, don't fight anyone twice your size, he said with a glowing smile."

I thought in that split second that Little Harry's acne problem seemed to disappear when that big smile came on.

"I don't know why we fought so much, but we did," Little Harry said.

I was ready to reply with my rosy words of wisdom when a voice boomed out.

"Atten-hut."

That got our attention, but we didn't know if someone was playing a joke on us.

Chapter Four

"Atten-hut," the voice barked.

We jumped to our own version of attention.

"Line up in rows of three. Move."

Suddenly my arm was grabbed and I was pulled to the side. I was ready to pull my arm away when The Voice said I was the third rank and the line up started to my left.

The second and first ranks started just ahead of me as this man was yanking us in line.

"Move. Move. Move."

The assembly was forming into a phalanx of worn out and tired bodies, but not as fast as The Voice wanted.

"Move. Move. Move. When you're in rank, line up straight left and right at an arm's length and keep your distance from the rank in front of you with an extended arm. Mark your distance in front to the longest arm length.

In as little as 10 seconds clumping feet fell silenced and we were in place as if he had willed us there.

Together for our first military assembly, we faced our Training Instructor, a.k.a. Sergeant Douglas Hardin, who did not look like The Voice who panicked us. The sergeant looked to be in his mid-30s, dark wavy hair and easy to look at. There was nothing intimidating about him in stature or manner but the command in his voice that exacted what he wanted.

"The only words I want to hear from you are 'Yes, Sergeant.'" His eyes were not unfriendly, but certainly not comforting in that moment.

"Do you understand?"

Rather than reply, we stood silent. "DO YOU UNDERSTAND?" he shouted without appearing to shout.

"Yes, sir," we shot back at him in a roar, self-satisfied.

"I am not an officer. I am not called sir. I am your Training Instructor. I am a sergeant. DO YOU UNDERSTAND?"

"Yes, sergeant."

"Somehow I am not impressed with your collective

intelligence. The next time anyone calls me "sir" they will wish they hadn't. Furthermore, I am not your father, or your mother. Nor am I your girlfriend, so do not attempt to fuck me."

That brought some grins and even a few titters, but Sgt. Hardin seemed to ignore them until he moved through our mass and stopped in front of Estaban, who apparently was eyeing the sergeant.

"Eyes straight ahead. Do not follow me. I am everywhere. I see everything"

He turned away, but quickly snapped back toward Estaban.

"Were you doing something I would approve of, or would you by any chance want to fuck me like I told you not to?" His dark penetrating eyes and direct tone cut off any motion from those close to them. My vision was blocked slightly, but I could see Estaban trying to keep from grinning, fighting for control.

I felt a sudden concern. It could easily have been me trying to keep from grinning. As a prankster, sometimes caught for my mischievous pranks, I found myself trying not to laugh when confronted by an authority figure, the prank still roiling in my mind.

Sgt. Hardin turned and began walking along the rank. I heard a snicker but couldn't tell who made it. Sgt. Hardin stopped and turned back towards Estaban. Then in the same pattern as before he stopped, turned and eyed Estaban.

"I don't want you in my flight. You are dismissed."

Estaban was as stunned as the rest of us. I was sure the sergeant was deadly serious, like when my dad brought out the whipping belt, but I doubted Estaban was the one who snickered.

"Didn't you hear me? You can leave. NOW."

"What, I mean, where should I go?" said Estaban, his voice sickly.

"I don't care. Just leave. Do whatever you were doing before you got here. You look like a surfer. Go back to surfing, You must like that more than paying attention to what I say."

"I am sorry, sergeant. I don't want to leave."

"But I have dismissed you already. That means you have to leave whether or not you want to."

"But sergeant, I just can't, I mean , I, uh, I don't." His voice was a plaintive plea and we could all hear his voice cracking, and I could see his dark eyes blinking. He was fighting back tears. His lips quivered and his body began to sway.

Sgt. Hardin stood rigidly, his eyes transfixed on Estaban.

As tense seconds passed I felt a smoldering anger rising up in me. I'd felt the frequent hurt of being treated unfairly and its wounds were deep, the scarring a constant reminder that I was considered less important than others. I felt victimized by this barrage. My mind was swarming with disapproval, and yet something much deeper wavered within me. I felt it circling within me quietly like a whisper in a budding tornado. I had a sudden intuitive understanding pressing me to do something out of character. The pressure mounted in spite of the danger. As I had struck out against it for myself, I knew, at this juncture, that I could not stand there without doing something to stop this painful display. I feared for my budding friend and whoever was next.

"Sergeant Hardin," I croaked, trying to keep my emotions stilled. My voice startled many, who twisted to see who dared speak. I could see their movement, but I tried to see Sgt. Hardin and if he was coming toward me.

"You are not moving," Sgt. Hardin said quietly to Estaban. "Are you disobeying my order to leave, or do you want someone to go with you?"

I knew then I was tapped as the one way escort. I waited in the quiet seconds that stretched out and expected that others were holding their breaths awaiting my demise.

"I'll go," said Estaban, in resignation, even though

his jaw jutted out in defiance.

He began to turn to his left, where there were fewer recruits standing at attention. As he moved slightly away, Sgt. Hardin told him to take his duffel bag.

"Take them as souvenirs of what could have been."

As much as this disgrace would probably haunt me the rest of my life, I could not stop myself.

"Sergeant Hardin," I blurted. "Can I leave, too? What he did or didn't do, I did, too. I feel just as much disrespect as he showed you if you felt that way."

"My, my, that was a mouthful," Sgt. Hardin said dryly.

"You there, the one walking away," he added. You can come back."

In that instant I felt relief for Estaban, even knowing I was the new target of whatever point he was making to the rest of them and my emotions settled. A calmness came over me, even though I had been here often and knew what was to come.

I saw Sgt. Hardin move to my side of the phalanx and weave his way to the back where I stood. How he could tell where I was, I figured, was instinct, or he had a built-in radar for noise in the ranks. He stopped by the young man next to me, who was quick to respond, "Not me, sergeant."

Sgt. Hardin smiled as he turned directly to me. He latched onto my eyes with open amusement.

"What's your name?" cooed the dagger in his voice.

"Breckenridge, sergeant."

"That was an impressive speech, young man." Do you know that boy?"

"No, sergeant," I lied.

"So you defy me in defense of someone who you don't know. Why would you do that? Are you planning to be bunk buddies? Does he remind you of your little brother? Please answer one or more of my questions? Have any of them hit the proverbial mark?

"No, Sgt. Hardin." I could have stopped right there, but I wanted to tell him how unfairness hurts. Some anger came out of the calm, it rose steadily like a tapped well.

"You're not even close," I said.

"No, Breckenridge, you're not even close." He paused for that extra moment to gain greater attention to what he was going to say next.

"If you plan to get out of the military, if that was your intention, you have failed miserably. I look forward to you being my favorite trainee. And I will measure this flight on your performance. If you do poorly, they will pay for it. And then you will pay for it, if you get my drift.

Before I could reply, Sgt. Hardin thrust out his hand and pointed it in my face. "And when I want something done, you will be my first choice for doing it. How does that sound?"

"Generous, sergeant."

"I give you credit, you are quick." He executed a snappy about face and weaved through his charges. Back in front, he reacted as if our exchange had never occurred, nor that Estaban was back with us.

"I am your sergeant, who knows what is best for you and will make sure you understand I know best. What I want to hear from you is silence. Anyone who feels the need to talk, unless asked a question, will find out how unhappy I can get. If you have any questions, keep them to yourself. Do you understand?"

"Yes, sergeant," came our dutiful reply.

"When I call your name, simply say, 'here.' Nothing else. Not yes, or anything other than 'here.'" If I mispronounce your name, correct me. It will be the only time in the next six weeks you will correct me. Because I know best."

Looking down at his clipboard, Sgt. Hardin began calling off names. Suddenly I became acutely aware how much different we all were, from clothing to speech to attitudes to how much we were alike, facing the same challenge, to be molded into a military person who followed orders despite our differences. It also dawned on me that he had passed up my name. He was up to Miller, who yelled "here," and onward until he asked if anyone's name was missed. Before I could reply, he cut me off.

"I know what you are thinking. I forgot Breckenridge. How could I forget Breckenridge? He's my favorite trainee. And being my favorite, your first duty, Breckenridge, will be to carry this clipboard." As he continued, he walked slowly through the ranks toward me. "Every place we go, you will have it signed by the duty sergeant before we enter and after we leave. If you forget the clipboard and we miss our mess, or lose our clipboard, something will happen that you will not soon forget. Your fellow trainees here will exact the necessary punishment in order to improve your sense of responsibility."

As he approached me he said, "Is that clear?" Without looking at me he handed me the clipboard, and continued onto the front of the flight squad.

It wasn't what I expected, this clipboard duty. What unnerved me was the "necessary punishment" due me if I messed up. Stubby's punch was still a painful reminder of exacted punishment. What others may have in store for me for a similar infraction was worrisome. As a

fledgling newsboy the ritual hazing had left me
emotionally scarred by the meanness of others, while
they considered it playful. I hid the bruises as best I
could from my parents but never forgot their looks as
they meted out their punishment on me.

We marched in raggedy fashion left, right, left right,
toward the processing building, where I was summoned
to sign us in. I broke ranks clumsily, bumping into
another trainee and apologizing for it.

"Stop right there," Sgt. Harding blurted as he moved
in on me.

As he approached me he didn't have the determined
look I was now getting use to seeing up close. However,
his movement was calculated to draw attention. He
barely looked at me.

"Breckenridge's bumbling moves are bothersome to
me, and when something or someone bothers me, I
correct it.

I expected the worst, but again he ignored me.

"Our first lesson will be on disengagement from the
ranks.

To me, he said, "Follow me."

Now he had me in front of everyone. I was sure my
punishment would be humiliating. I stopped and
followed his instruction for where to stand.

Sgt. Hardin ordered them to turn to him in what was a ragged left face.

"Watch what I do with my feet." He executed a left face. Then a right face. And an about face. "You," he pointed to me, "Do the same. Show them you have been paying attention."

I mimicked his movements, right down to keeping my thumbs on my pant seams.

"Very good. Since Breckenridge has shown you how to do these simple movements, you will show me how you were paying attention to him.

"Left face," he shouted.

They turned, every which way, and not smartly.

"Did I not show you how to make these simple turns, and did not Breckenridge show you?"

Yesses and noes reverberated in the cool air.

"While Breckenridge here will sign us in, we will learn our left from our right and execute very simple turns. Do you know your left from your right? Please tell me you do?"

"Yes sergeant," they shouted.

I left as his commands split the crisp air and I tried not to smile when he immediately raged at those who turned right. When I returned minutes later, their movements were executed smartly. Sgt. Hardin wasn't displeased when I returned. Even I was pleased.

Into the process center we went, beginning what would plague us for the remainder of our enlistment: the hurry up and wait procedure of bureaucracy life.

For the remainder of the day we plodded from one station to another for registration, medical checkups (cough), a brief mess, haircuts that left us sheared to baldness, clothing and equipment procurement, and finally a full mess before we were marched with duffle bags over our shoulders to barracks No. 8012 as Flight 1416.

Chapter Five

Marching on the way to our barracks, with our shaved heads bobbing in the ranks, I recognized that first step in our metamorphosis. With our shaved heads, who could tell who was a surfer, a New York wise ass, or a fuckup as I assumed I was considered, aside from our attire. And once that was set aside, the look would put us together on the same bottom rank, until once more we would begin to assert ourselves or exist in anonymity.

Our barracks, like all the barracks we passed, reminded me of a large white barn. There were five barracks on each side of the passageway, which was about the width of an alley. Ours was the fourth one down on the right or the second one on the left depending on which road you took to get there. A railing and a set of two steps below an outside light again reminded me of my early life on a farm. I felt comfortable gazing at it, this temporary home for six weeks, but I couldn't quite get the nervousness out of my system. It conjured up the discomfort I felt in going from a large urban high school to a farm community high school in my sophomore year. It took me a couple of days to get over the looks I received, as if I were an unknown specimen of unknown origin. Eventually it worked out, but I never forgot the breaking in period and I supposed it would be the same here, too. We were after all just like a class of high school kids, minus the girls, feeling out each other to see where we fit: as leadership, the followers and wannabes, and the alienated, for a variety of reasons. I guessed I was bound for the alienated, but the reason was known: Sgt. Hardin.

The barracks itself comprised two floors, the same bottom and top. Latrines were on one side, an open day room and a separate room for the TI on the opposite corner. An open bay occupied the remainder, with roughly 30 bunks on each side. The bunks were two-high, upper and lower.

When we entered, Sgt. Hardin read off names and I became aware of something I doubt anyone noticed, but would sooner or later. Sgt. Hardin was separating us into groupings of his own making, even though he was calling out names in alphabetical order. The surfers were split up evenly as were the East Coasters and the farm boys and the remainder. He was setting the stage for natural selection of a who's who within the flight.

The first of many challenges for who eventually would rule amongst ourselves came in the choosing of bunks, lower and upper.

It didn't really matter to me one way or the other. Without any thought about it I threw my burdensome duffel bag on a bottom bunk, glad to be rid of its heaviness.

Someone else did the same in the bunk next to mine, and I thought of being neighborly and passing along a kind "hi neighbor." As I turned toward him, Stubby's bulk came into view and swiftly grabbed the duffel bag of my neighbor and tossed it into the aisle.

"What the fuck you doing?" said the young neighbor, slight of build like myself.

His look was of unprovoked disbelief, anger, and innocence.

"I already got dibs on this," Stubby said in his hard, bullying voice.

"I got here first," said the kid, now annoyed and bending to grab his duffel bag.

"Naw, you can take another one. I like this one. It's mine."

My not about to be new neighbor rose with the duffel bag in hand and twisted toward Stubby, who stood in front of him like a massive pillar. I could see my ex-neighbor was aware of the sudden quiet overcoming the bay, including those still coming into the lower bay. There must have been a palpable tension in the air that human instinct picked up. I felt it and looked across the bay toward expectant faces. Dan'l Boone, his golf ball sized Adam's Apple a trait of leadership stood silently, a sad, tired look in his face that belied intervention. Was nobody going to stand up for the lad, who had by now begun to redden as Stubby glared at him contemptuously?

The kid tried to toss the heavy bag back onto the cot, and repossess it, but Stubby swiped the bag away, which pulled the lad and the bag sideways toward me. I had to step aside to avoid being hit, but staring at them made me slow to act. The duffel bag hit me and nearly knocked me down. A couple of guys laughed, which only got the lad angrier. He let go of the bag, which I now had control of, and turned back to see what would happen next.

"It's mine. I told you I got here first," the lad said, liquid in its innocence despite his anger.

"Too bad."

"You can't do this."

"I am. It's mine," said Stubby, turning his back to the kid and unbuckling his bag and taking out clothing.

The soon to be ex-neighbor hadn't made up his mind what to do as the others seemed to know that his efforts were futile and went about their own business. He stood there devastatingly alone and abandoned of any support. He knew if he wanted the cot, he would have to take on Stubby, but I could see he was unwilling to do that. He stood there mute in the middle of the aisle as the incoming throng now brushed by him and settled themselves without any new hassles. The stupefied lad, seconds past his humiliation suddenly seemed to feel he had to move and in doing so realized he had to find another bunk. He turned awkwardly, eyes searching for a haven, only to get dissenting nods. None were available. Except for one. Only one bunk was empty of a duffel bag: the top over Stubby.

The kid saw that as had most of everyone else. Wearily, as if physically spent, my soon to be neighbor dragged his bag over to my side of the bunk away from Stubby. Without a word, he began unpacking his duffel bag. Stubby was ignoring him until his reluctant bunk mate stepped on the side of Stubby's bunk to get up to his cot.

"Hey, what you doing?" he shouted, catching the attention of everyone and stopping the kid. "Git down. Git.

The kid lowered himself to the floor.

"You don't step on my bed. No. You gotta go up the back. There," he said. pointing to the back metal bracing of the bunks.

Already beaten, the kid stepped up on the back brace and pulled himself over the top brace to get to the top bunk. Without a word, he settled on his back and just laid there, never to be heard from again.

I on the other hand was surprised to find out who was my bunk buddy. It was Estaban.

"Hey," I said in a hello, when I turned to see him easily mount the bracing and bounce atop. He nestled in while looking down at me, a delightful smile on his face. Then left hand came out in a stretch toward me. I grasped his hand with my left hand and we shook. "Estaban, Estaban Leeds, my friend."

By the time I got into my bunk, dried from my shower and tooth brushing, I was spent and looking forward to a deep slumber until roused at six a.m., according to some know it alls. Unfortunately they didn't know it all. Somewhere in my dream someone was making a very loud noise, an ear splitting, nerve wracking, eye opening din. The noise continued as I awoke and saw pandemonium all around me. Then the reason for this madness was crystallized in someone yelling: "Fire Drill. Fire Drill." My God, the building was on fire, my mind told me. It apparently was asleep with me. It looked like an Americanized Chinese Fire Drill. Everyone was milling about in their own stupors when suddenly the noise stopped and Sgt. Hardin's voice boomed out. "This is a fire drill. There will be NO TALKING as you leave the barracks. Lower bay will go out the rear door and assemble at attention in an orderly fashion. Upper bay is going out the front door and assembling there. There is no fire. If there had been a fire, you would have all burned to death by being so slow. I repeat: NO TALKING. Now get moving.

And we did. Not orderly, but we got out in the very cold air, which numbed most of us. We tried to sort out ourselves in an assembly, but without talking it was an insurmountable task. I was milling about, the cold nearly suffocating me when I was startled to hear someone blurt out: "Damn, it's cold."

And it wasn't me this time. Johnny on the spot, an unknown sergeant, who we later found out was part of the fire drill at a neighboring barracks, swooped into us searching for the talker.

"Who spoke out?" he said, forcing himself into our throng. We all turned mutely toward his voice but moved away from it. He was like a fire burning everything in his path.

Except for Stubby.

Shivering, callously numbed by the cold and a rude awakening, he blurted, "Shit. It's too damn cold," as he flapped his hands on his arms to create warmth.

Shining like a beacon, Stubby was dead meat. The sergeant rushed up to him and before he could berate him, Stubby was undaunted in his complaint. "What the fuck we doin' this for?"

"Why are you talking? You have been told not to talk. You are in a world of shit, do you hear me?"

Stubby remained unfazed by the onslaught. As he shivered he looked around him, through and past the sergeant directly in front of him. Like a heat-seeking missile, he grabbed out for a brown blanket draped over another recruit. Stubby wrenched the blanket off the boy, who was startled.

"Hey, that's mine," he blurted.

Immediately the sergeant turned to the boy and shouted "You have been told not to talk. Why are you talking? You are in a world of shit."

No one seemed to know what to do with the windup toy sergeant, who was now glaring at the shivering blanketless boy.

"What's going on here?" The now familiar voice of Sgt. Hardin entered the fray.

"These boys of yours broke silence," the sergeant said.

"Which ones?"

"These two," he said, grabbing the t-shirt of the Blanketless One and stretching out to grab Stubby.

"Keep your hands off me," spat Stubby, hardly contrite for someone in deep shit.

In our first pleasant surprise category, Sgt. Hardin then commanded the other sergeant to release the

Blanketless One.

The sergeant was taken aback by Hardin's summary dismissal and it showed. It was as if someone had breached a jurisdiction or protocol, but I was not sure who had done it. "It's my mess. I'll clean it up."

"You better, Hard On" the sergeant barked, visibly annoyed and turning away.

"Everyone back in the barracks except for you two," Hardin said harshly. "Give me that," he said, grabbing the blanket and pulling it off Stubby.

I didn't hear any protest as I was nudged back into the barracks. I wanted to stick around and see what punishment was going to be meted out, but Daniel Boone's large hand was pressing me away. His face was telling me I best move on. Once inside, everyone scurried to the warmth of their bunks. I waited for them to come back in, but sleep overcame me.

Again my slumber was interrupted by someone yelling. "Rise and shine. Let's go, let's go." Hardin had become everyone's nemesis. The grousing didn't let up until we had finished the ritual shit, shower and shave, although the last was not necessary on me. Or so I thought.

"Get 'em all, boy," said one of Boone's angular buddies, peering at my face and pointing out some light hairs that I hadn't even noticed. He offered his Gillette.

Then he instructed me on the art of the good shave – to feel the face without looking at it.

"Started shavin' at eight," he said as he watched my fledgling attempts at not cutting myself, but only the hairs, some of which eluded me at every swipe. "Agin the grain," he said, showing me. I admit I liked his manner. He was no longer just backwoods dumb and ready to fight at any whim. I began to respect his ways and asked his name, turning away from the mirror as I scraped my face. "Bodeen," he said, and winced. as my blood emerged from a slight cut. "You don't get the feel, you'll be wearing a lot of toilet paper." He handed me a spot of paper to stanch the blood flow. He looked at my face closely and said you'll do.

Back out in the bay, dressing in our new attire, green fatigues, which I thought made us look like gardeners, had commenced. Most of the comments did little justice to what the Air Force considered appropriate attire – for working. This work aspect had been overlooked until Boone pointed it out to us. "Now you know what you're here for. This is not just a training camp. This is a working place"

"How do you know so much?" asked one of my unnamed brethren.

"Paying attention -- and keeping my mouth shut, which I suggest y'all make a habit."

"What's your name, old man?" asked one of the

surfers I recognized after the haircuts.

"Jeremiah Hennessey, Oak Hill, Tennessee. And you?"

"Darren Wylie, Malibu. That's in Cal if or ni a."

It could've stopped there, but something had been tapped into, not just touched on, and it caught on, and I felt that it was what separated us from all the other flights we encountered during our training. We wanted to know about each other early on, find a familiarity that we could rely on and hold on to when things got rough, as we all expected would happen. Wylie had come out from his anonymity and picked up on it. "And you," he said pointing to Bodeen.

"Zachary Bodeen, Little Oak, Tennessee. And you?"

He was pointing at me.

"Jon Breckinridge, Allen Park, Michigan," I said, and pointed to another and said, "And you?"

It bounced about the room like a rubber ball, being caught by all but a few, who in their own ways would stay anonymous because they were not originally sought out or whose inclination was singularity.

A tall gaunt Cajun, whose comment: "This ain't the Boy Scouts" tossed the ball out the window. Those overlooked were stranded or easily sank back in their comfortable anonymity. As I was to learn later on, one person just like that was unforgettable, and not likened to friendship.

We marched to chow in our own haphazard display, bundled up in our fatigue jackets as the crisp north wind lashed us. Despite Sgt. Hardin's cadence counts, we lacked a rhythm. We bounced along like bobbers on a pond, some losing step, which caused others to misstep. We were so disjointed I was embarrassed to be part of it. Prior to our return from our breakfast, Sgt. Hardin explained the simplicity he wanted. Left foot, right foot, left, right, left right. Someone chuckled.

"This is not funny, it's pathetic," barked Sgt. Hardin. You walk like you've got poles stuck up your asses. Keep it up and I'll shove some deeper. Do you understand?"

"Yes, sergeant," we barked back.

The weather gave no reprieve from this onerous task as the cold northerly wind scoured our faces. The darkened sky had soft clouds scurrying southward as we marched in the other direction. And there was this smell that rolled in with the cold. I didn't know which was worse, the frigid wind or the smell of something dead. At that point, I figured it for a tie. Only later did I find out it was a horse slaughterhouse, but even knowing that it didn't diminish the sickly smell of blood. It was a smell that stayed with you and when the doors of the abattoir were opened to air out the slaughtering, it was infectious and stuck to the memory, now 50 years later.

Back at the barracks, Sgt. Hardin began delegating responsibilities to a chosen foursome, Squad Leaders, who had the burden of keeping individual ranks working as a unit, in drill or in work duties and make sure those duties and tasks were done as he wanted them.

From our bay he chose Hennessey and a surfer named Hewitt. I understood the choice of Jeremiah, but Hewitt was a total surprise. His only attribute was his height. Later I would understand. Squad Leaders marched up front. Sgt. Hardin assembled us in a tapered phalanx, from taller to smaller. This symmetry looked streamline and cohesive and would allow familiarity with those around us, like birds of a feather.

The other two Squad Leaders were Kent Berrywood and John Smalls. Smalls, I later discovered was from Detroit. A tall barrel chested lug, who I faintly remembered seeing on the train, brightened as his name was called.

I enjoyed the training, although some groused silently. We learned how to tightly make our cots. The test was to flip a coin on the blanket. If it bounced, it was right. Our footlocker contents had to be arranged in a particular way. Everything had to be done in a specific way. Everything had to be sharp looking and clean, including us. Sgt. Hardin explained his inspections and squadron inspections would be made regularly, and gigs, – military vernacular for demerits – handed out for things not done properly. Sufficient demerits could place some in jeopardy of extra duties, or worse, being booted out of the service.

Stubby and the Blanketless One already had gotten gigs for the fire alarm incident. I expected Sgt. Hardin to come up to me at any time and issue gigs from my Day One outburst. Then the day came. We had been outside policing the area around the barracks, picking up whatever was strewn by the wind or carelessly thrown by others, when I was told to report to Sgt. Hardin. What had I done?

Chapter Six

I knocked on Sgt. Hardin's door while the front door guard gestured with one hand high and his neck bent. I gave him the finger.

Told to enter, I did. Sgt. Hardin was polishing his brogans while sitting at a table. The cleaning paraphernalia was spread out on the table. Included was a bottle of rubbing alcohol. Here in his own familiar surroundings he looked different. Like a man in his den enjoying a football game on television. Warm and settled in.

I tried to relax while at attention.

He took his time polishing, and I watched intently. Sporadically, he applied some alcohol to his blackened cloth and dabbed it around the toe.

After finishing one brogan, he looked at it with satisfaction, and spoke.

"You can use your own spit, or rubbing alcohol, but make sure if you have some you put it in your footlocker, to the right. You know where."

I did. And nodded.

"I need someone I can depend on, someone to do a job for me."

Many thoughts swirled in my mind, mostly negative. Chief was being volunteered to do something I didn't want to do.

"Don't look so worried. At ease."

I rested my bunched shoulders.

"The duty roster outside has to be filled out daily. I need someone to do it for me."

I was stunned. The implication was overwhelming.

Without looking up, he said, "Are you willing to do it?"

Who was this guy imitating Sgt. Hardin, a.k.a. Hard-On? Certainly not the sergeant who relished reaming our asses at every misstep.

"Yes, yes sir, I mean, yes, sergeant."

"Let's keep it our secret." He twirled his cloth in circles, covering the leather with precision. "You can keep a secret can't you?"

"How would I go about doing this without being

seen?"

"You have free time. Figure it out. Get with me after you do."

It was like giving me a key to the chastity belt. I paused in the doorway, about to make another mistake when the sergeant saved me.

"Don't take this as any familiarity between us. You caught me in a good mood that first day. Otherwise I would have personally washed you out and enjoyed every minute of it. Close the door on your way out."

As I exited the sergeant's room, the door guard made the gesture again. I repeated my own and swept passed him. I was giddy with the excitement of having something rare, something of value that could make my life easier during basic training. I saw Jeremiah and wanted to let someone know of my windfall. I approached him as he scuffed his brogan across the grass. He bent over and picked up a toothpick. He gazed at it, then at me. His countenance said he was wise to something.

I tried to be casual. Then he smiled. That full grin with large teeth and long angular nose and those blue eyes in a ruddy face was so appealing I had to smile back.

"Since I don't see a pole up your ass, you came away with something."

"Yeah, sorta." Something began to bother me. Telling was not a good idea, even though Jeremiah was ramrod straight about things. To do this as a secret meant no one should know. I didn't know if I was strong enough to not tell someone. If no one knew then it was like it had not happened at all. That quandary must have shown on my face.

"You want something from me, or, have something for me," he said in that honest-to-goodness manner.

The weight of the secret was just too burdensome to carry alone. I hesitated, still unsure what this kind of power really meant. It was the way he looked at me, his head tilted off to the side, like my dog Whiskey, whose loyalty was unquestionable, that sold me.

"For you. But it's got to be a secret between us, and I mean only us."

"It's that good?"

I told him and he stopped grinning. What I wanted was a pinch of glory for having that smidgen of power. What I told him was that I wanted his input on the slackers and the troublemakers. "You know, guys who deserve punishment."

"There's only a few and you know who they are, so why bring me in on this?"

"The other bay. You've got friends."

Jeremiah put his hand on his chin in what appeared to be his heavy thinking mode.

I knew I had better be sharp. Telling suddenly became a burden just as much as not telling weighed heavily on me.

Jeremiah stopped massaging his chin. "Can you do something for me?"

"Who?"

"You are quick. Bo doesn't like cleaning toilets. And …"

"Whoa. Christmas was last month."

"Just checking to see what you were going to do with this.

I felt like I was playing a game of chess and a slight anxiety rose up in my gut. What was my next best move? One thing was for sure. I didn't like preferential treatment, which came from being the middle child. Had I recognized that the core of my existence to this point was getting attention from those I wanted it from? If so, it wasn't enough. There had to be more and I had to figure out what else was important. "I" wasn't the issue." I was back to Square One. My dilemma.

"No one is exempt. We all do duty. You, me, Bo, all of us.

"Otherwise we become suspicious."

"Exactly."

"So how do you get the names to Sgt. Hardin?"

I knew that answer when Sgt. Hardin offered me the job

"A drop box."

"A what?"

"A place where he can pick it up without me being there. A mail box, sorta. I read a lot of spy novels."

"Did that when Lucinda and I started out. Her pappy didn't like my family so we had to meet on the sly. Used the Tinners' mailbox for our messages. The Tinners stayed inside. They was old. Lucinda took them their mail."

"How old are you, if you don't mind me asking?"

"Twenty six. We been together going on 10 years. Twin boys, Thad and Nate, age six."

"You're not married?"

"Yea-uh, we are, homestyle."

Jeremiah handed me a picture from his wallet. It showed him standing tall and angular with her laid back against him and two blond haired tykes standing on both sides of them. And she was as beautiful a woman as I have ever seen. Movie star like and big breasted, a combination that easily won me over.

"Damn. You are one lucky guy. She's beautiful."

"I know it."

"So why are you in the military? Aren't you exempt?

"We been living together. No real license. Same as my parents.

Damn. I couldn't get over how beautiful she was, absolutely gorgeous. My estimation of Jeremiah soared. "Doesn't really matter," I muttered, imagining what she looked like without clothes. I must have been imagining for too long when Jeremiah broke through my reverie.

His drop box, I proposed, would be my fatigue jacket's left pocket, which would be left unsnapped. The jacket was hung in the open just to the right of a window. "Whenever you have names, write 'em down and put them in the left pocket. Those guys will be on the next latrine or KP roster.

"The what?"

"KP. Kitchen patrol. Kitchen duty. I found that out from the mess sergeant. We're all supposed to do it. A whole day. I mean eight hours. Washing dishes.

"I don't do dishes," Jeremiah stated emphatically.

There it was, the sticking point that could ruin the master plan. It was now my time to paw the ground with my brogan. My thoughts returned to my mother. Old world Italian. She wouldn't relent when I complained about my chores. They were tasks of effort to her, responsibility to my father. It was part of everyday life.

When I stopped pawing the ground, I looked up into Jeremiah's face, not directly making eye contact, and imparted my father's favorite saying prior to getting a spanking: "It won't hurt for long." I patted Jeremiah on the arm and turned away resolutely. And hoping for no retort.

None came. With great relief I went back into the barracks.

Rarely did the routine of basic training change. Formerly my mother's insistence was presently Sgt. Hardin's demands. Make your bed, clean your area, follow orders. The monotonous drill of it would eventually transform us into the minions of military life. That transition occurred with boring regularity except for some memorable incidents.

Early on two new recruits were discharged for medical problems overlooked by recruitment doctors: One for flat feet, the other for an ear problem. When Stubby, who never seemed to recover from his hate of the cold, was washed out as unfit for military duty, we realized we were all in jeopardy

One in particular was marked from the start. Freddie Forteneau, the tall, gaunt Cajun. He had the messy bunk next to me. He wouldn't make his cot right, then his brogans weren't shined enough. Each daily inspection was a test for us, but Forteneau laughed it all off or reminded us he wasn't a boy scout. Each of these meant demerits not only for Forteneau, but the entire flight, which in the long run would hurt our chances to get out of the barracks and move about the base on our own.

When I commented on his messiness, he told me to fuck off. End of conversation. When a squad leader told him to shape up, Forteneau told him to mind his own business. When Sgt. Hardin said it was time for the squad leaders to take control of the barracks, the meaning was clearer to some than to others. For my part, my parents would have been overwhelmed had they known that I spent all of my evenings making sure that my area was spotless, my clothing and footlocker neat and shoes perfectly shined. I didn't have any time for conversations, about Forteneau or anything else. For the first time in my life, I had a purpose: not to get in any more trouble and avoid demerits.

That night, I remember, I was particularly tired and quickly fell asleep. Sometime in the middle of the night I had a dream -- with noises. It was perplexing until I realized the noises, muffled groans and thumping sounds, didn't fit the dream. The dream turned into a nightmare when someone brushed against me and I abruptly awoke. The moaning sounds didn't stop. My eyes turned to the sounds cloaked in irregular darkness. For a reason unknown the bay's night light had been turned off. I heard the thumping again as my eyes adjusted to the darkness. I saw dark shapes around Freddie's cot and then a lump under a blanket being held tight by two shapes while other shapes were slamming something into the lump. What I saw was now horrible, reminiscent of piranhas feasting on something or someone. Even when I recognized what was happening, I couldn't respond. The furious flurry of attack stunned me. I was afraid of moving, lest the attack turn on me, so I watched the horror as others whispered, asking to partake in what I later found out was a "bunk beating." Then someone said that was enough. But the moaning continued well into the night until I fell asleep. It was a fitful sleep. Something dark was following me.

I awoke feeling oddly out of place, cold and damp rather than warm and nestled in. It felt like I was back in the crappy hotel that housed us fledgling Boy Scouts for the night in a bizarre trip to Chicago. It was supposed to be an adventure, but it turned into a nightmarish carousal of trouble making scouts from Evansville, Ill., who harassed everyone and kept our unsupervised troop awake the whole dingy night. Boy Scouts my ass. They were hoodlums. The thoughts of them bursting into our room and flushing us out with threats of mayhem haunted me for years afterward. It had been a long time since that particular nightmare emerged. Yet a cold shiver reminded me of that nightmare and I listened to the sounds around me to get a sense of where I was.

"Come on, get your lazy butt up," someone said close to me. I pulled my blanket over my head for more warmth and security. Suddenly my cot was jarred. Abruptly awakened, I expected to see a menacing Chicago hoodlum hovering over me, brandishing a knife. Even as that thought emerged, it angered me. I was pissed and bolted out of my cot.

Darren gaped as I lunged into him. Actually I stumbled and crashed into him.

"What the fuck," he said as he shoved me away from him.

Again I stumbled and was about to crash into something else when I was caught and twisted into an erect stance. Jeremiah's strong hands held my shoulders.

"Whoa, there," he said paternally.

Recognition brought me out of my nightmarish fit and it felt like home. Fully awake, the bay's early morning commotion comforted me.

"Thanks, for the catch."

"You okay," he cooed like my mom.

"Yup. Thanks again. Musta had a bad night."

"Not as bad as Freddie boy," chortled Bo.

I twisted to look over at Freddie's bunk. A lump remained where I had seen it in my dream. What instantly drew me to it, I don't know. Slowly, quietly I approached the lump. I nudged it. "Forteneau?"

An arm came slashing out at me. I jumped back.

"Get away," came a coarse growl.

I stared at the wavering arm, reddish brown bruises dappling it.

"Frank? Are you okay?"

Again, the coarse growl.

As I moved away, Bo and squad leader Jimmy Hewitt yelled for Freddie to get up.

"Fuck you."

It was no longer a coarse growl, but a pained one.

Bo yanked the blanket off Freddie, who was curled up in a fetal position and shivering, although I wasn't sure it was from the cold alone.

"Get your mangy ass out of bed, Forteneau," Hewitt yelled.

The barrack's sounds silenced. Everyone in the bay turned to Freddie's cot. I could see the smirks of pleasure on many faces and with each I visualized a brogan in hand. In that instant, something changed in me. It hadn't occurred as a hazed newsboy, but now older I recognized the pleasure of their assault. What they enjoyed disgusted me. Justified or not, I knew I would never do that to another and I felt that separation of me from them. Given the right set of circumstances, they were all piranhas waiting to feast on someone. I wanted nothing to do with them. I felt the change in me so profoundly, I knew this is what growing up was all about. I seemed to feel my thin skin thickening. A hardening was sweeping through me to coat every organ and nerve. It was steadying me for my next disappointment and how I would react to it.

I turned to Jeremiah and was relieved to see his own disappointment. He caught my eye and shook his head sadly. I panned my eyes across the bay, looking for other sympathetic faces when Estaban whispered in my ear. "I heard it last night. They really beat the hell outa him."

A flash of the beating came back to me, and as much as I was again repulsed by it, another feeling surfaced. It arose in me like regurgitated bile. It was my own shame for not having done something and it had the taste of self-contempt. Even as I recalled my fear of their attack I understood I had shirked a moral responsibility. I had acted out of cowardice and a shudder pulsed through me and surfaced.

"Yeah, I got the same feeling," Estaban said.

I wanted to tell him what I was shuddering from, to

set the record straight, but my normal candor shut down. What I had just perceived as a hint of gained maturity now was a loss to immaturity. I was separating from myself the person I wanted to be. Would I soon be bunk beating myself through self-loathing? I was trying to reset my moral compass when Sgt. Hardin's voice boomed.

"Let's get a move on," he said moving into the center of the bay. "Don't just stand there. Move," he ordered.

Quickly we responded. No one said anything or gestured to Freddie, who remained a lump under the blanket he had replaced over himself. Going to chow was an option, which meant some could stay in the sack until the others returned. Freddie's condition would be found out later. I felt relieved to be leaving, clipboard in hand.

When we returned to the barracks almost an hour later, we found Freddie missing. It was perplexing. Sgt. Hardin had marched us to the mess hall, and I was positive he had followed us in. He was outside the mess hall when we assembled to return to the barracks. Freddie was gone and with him all his possessions. Most startling was his bed was made, and made correctly. Never had a coin flopped on a bed Freddie made.

I never inquired as to his disappearance and no one imparted any information. Freddie Forteneau was no

more a part of our lives and his absence was not grist for
the rumor mills.

Chapter Seven

While Freddie was no more, someone replaced him rather quickly, someone so distinctly repulsive that I for one never forgot him, but for different reasons than the others in our flight.

We were in our third week of basic training and fitting snugly into our regular routine. We had begun to gel pretty well, having survived Sgt. Hardin's sneak inspections and responding well to his orchestration of orders. I had even had a conversation or two with the sergeant, which led me to believe he might be a human being. It was then that that term lost its meaning. We were going to get our mail at squadron headquarters. It was a daily occurrence, so nothing was anticipated out of the ordinary. As was often the case, another flight was there before us. As we marched up alongside them, we could tell they were fresh like ourselves, but unidentifiable.

They were standing alone at ease, stretched out in sideways formation, their squad leaders facing our squad leaders as we came to a halt beside them. Once we executed a right face, we looked like an elongated flight except for a four foot gap between us.

Sgt. Hardin put us at ease and went in to get the mail. It was one of the places we went that I didn't have to sign us in. I watched him as he got to the door, opened it, and then stopped. I thought he had forgotten something, when he flung his arm sideways as if stepping aside in a reverent manner. I didn't know if anyone else was witnessing this, but I was riveted to it. Sgt. Hardin didn't act like anyone who would step aside for another. He was his own man and someone who I had begun to respect. This incongruity had me focused and nervously awaiting the object of his subjugation. I could feel the drum roll play as Sgt. Hardin stood at attention while holding the door with his left index finger. Out of the darkness stepped a huge black sergeant holding a tray of letters. He filled the doorway, his head tilted as if to avoid bumping his head on the transom, and swept by without a nod. He was a specimen unlike anyone I had ever seen. He wore tailored green fatigues with the pants tapered and brogans shined like patent leather. He was disproportionate, with a large head, a huge gut and spindly legs, but wasn't ungainly. He moved so gracefully, he seemed to glide. He kept his eyes straight ahead as he approached his flight, while I was sure everyone of us were eyeballing him.

His big black face was dominated by a wide nose, bulbous red lips and small dark eyes that seemed to shine like his brogans. His thick neck rose up to tiny ears and a shaved head covered by a green fatigue hat. He was hideous and fearsome in his blackness, as if evil poured out from every pore. He reminded me of a gargoyle.

"Alrighty, alrighty. Let's see who's been a bad boy and who's been a good un. Didja all write your mommies like I told ya." His beady dark eyes glowed as he panned his audience like a probing camera, moving slowly one way and then the other. For an instant I was anxious that he might look directly at me and no doubt I would shrivel up under that malevolent gaze.

Then, as if he were a magician, letters were flying in the air like white birds. I heard him shout out names. At the call of every name another letter flew out of his hand. It was eerie to the point of being surreal. I was mesmerized by what I saw. Who was this hideous man who had birds flying out of his hands?

Then the shouting stopped and the birds stopped flying while his charges were scrambling for their mail like kids seeking candy from a broken piñata. Then someone was pushed trying to get his mail. The trainee sprawled out of ranks and nearly rammed into the sergeant's spindly legs. The sergeant ignored him and began letting more birds fly. The trainee tried to scramble back into the ranks amid flying letters. One flung letter hit a trainee near his eye. His arm lashed out in defense and struck the scrambling trainee, causing him to fall back again toward the sergeant.

We laughed. And then someone in the sergeant's flight laughed with us.

Suddenly the air turned cold. In a flash the sergeant moved like a cat upon his prey.

"Was so funny?" he said in a chilling voice as his dark face moved within inches of the laughing trainee's face.

The trainee, a sturdy white boy well over six feet tall and of muscular build, showed fear on his face. He seemed to be trying to overcome it by staying stiffly straight as the gigantic black sergeant loomed over him.

"Y'aren't peeing your pants, are ya?" The sergeant's face inched even closer.

The white boy's eyes darted about as the black sergeant's eyes bored into him.

"Yo momma take care of you boy, don't she? Yah, you know she does. And when youse feeling bad, she ease the pain wif a kiss. Yo momma ain't here, so I guess I gots to be your momma.

The trainee was now perceptibly shaking and trying to bend backward as the sergeant pressed his face forward. Then the black sergeant puckered his lips. I was now shaking, too, as the black sergeant kissed the white boy on the cheek. I shuddered and heard groans behind me and the whisper "nigger."

The sergeant withdrew his face, but just a few inches.

" Is I yo momma now, boy? No? Then I gots to do better. The groans from our flight grew louder as the black sergeant kissed the white boy on the lips and held them there for a couple of seconds. I was terrified, but my alarm was nothing compared to the outrage of the rednecks among us who whispered of getting even. As my mind reeled at the thought of what could happen because of this outrage, the black sergeant stepped back.

"Now you take care you don't disappoint yo momma again." In an instant he turned about and returned to the front of his flight. As consternated as I was, I caught the reappearance of Sgt. Harding, who stood nonchalantly on the steps of Command HQ, a tray of our letters in hand.

"Atten-hut," blared the black sergeant. Quickly his charges snapped to attention. I turned back to the punished trainee, who somehow had transformed himself into another shape, altogether different from the cowering lad of seconds past. "Left face, hut," he commanded. They snapped to the twist. "Six steps forward, march." They responded snappily, as if nothing had happened. Another maneuver and they were marching passed us.

"I'll get that nigger one way or the other," said an unrecognized voice in the flight.

"Oh, really," said a rarely heard calm voice of Sgt. Hardin. His quietness was disturbing and we expected some kind of onslaught. Instead he riffled through the letters in the basket he held. Seconds became tens of seconds. Then he looked up and smiled.

"It'll take ten of you to ruffle his feathers. Take heed. You have no idea what he is capable of."

This was not just one incident that would be forgotten in a week of adventures. That black man kissing that white boy on the lips scared me. I thought a lot about it and I wasn't the only one. Most of the white boys, especially from the South, surely wouldn't let it go.

When we got back to the barracks the heat, which had baked all the juices out of the leaves on the sapling next to the barracks, also withered the air in the barracks. My mouth felt like cotton.

"That nigger'd be strung up just like that," said Bo, with a snap of his fingers.

"I'd gut the fucker first," said Jimmy Hewitt, his face stern and unforgiving.

Since both were squad leaders, the whole bay appeared to side with them that first night after the incident occurred. It didn't make a difference where they came from, east, west, north or south, -- except for the few black trainees who nervously kept quiet about it -- the black sergeant was a nigger who deserved a first class whipping.

For my part, I kept silent until Bill Jopp sidled up to me, with a brogan and can of black shoe polish in hand. "What you think 'bout it, Breck?" he whispered, his back to Bo.

"What are you asking me, Jopp?" All I knew about him was that he lived in a ghetto somewhere in Chicago, and rarely spoke unless spoken to. I'd never had a conversation with him, nor even a passing hello.

"Well," he began in a regular tone so he could be heard if someone was listening, "my spit don't work on these shoe. Am I done something wrong?"

I waited for him to finish with "Massah" as he splayed his hands apart in supplication, his broad shoulders thick with heavy muscles and head drooped to his chest so he didn't eyeball me.

I thought to myself 'not a bad metaphor' for someone from the ghetto. He apparently felt threatened because he was a Negro. While mulling over a response, he spit on the shoe and started rubbing the surface with a wadded up piece of cloth, already smudged.

"Seems to me you're doing it right," I said, eyeing his circular motions on the black leather and thinking how to reply to the real question.

"'Member what they did to Freddie?" he whispered.

"Yah, but that was different, it was personal and he

was a fuckup," I responded in kind.

"So you don't think they be coming for us. What they did to him"

"Nah." But what did I know.

Jopp nodded awkwardly, his head twisting a bit. I knew someone was eavesdropping. Jopp's body was blocking him. I thought of peering sideways, but it didn't really matter who was there.

As my luck would have it, it was Mr. Instigator.

"What's going on?" Bo asked.

"Aren't you the inquisitive one. Fact is, it's a private conversation

"Bullshit. You're siding with the nigger. You a nigger lover, Jon?"

"I don't know any niggers, in the first place, and even if I did, I'd … "

"You're a nigger lover," he shouted. "I can't fucking believe it, this boy's a nigger lover," he shouted again and pointed at me.

I got angry. "Fuck you and what you believe."

Bo reached out for me as I clenched my fist. But Jeremiah got between us first.

"Hold on. Calm down," he eased us. Jeremiah turned to a captive audience. "Jon here is not a nigger lover because he don't know what the difference is between a black and a nigger.

"Yah, I do."

"No, you don't. You think you do, but you don't."

"So, what is it I don't understand?"

"There is no difference."

"That's right. You tell him, Jeremiah," Bo yelled amid a chorus of cheers.

"You mean you never had a colored friend that you wouldn't stand up for?" I eyed Jopp as I said it

"He'll turn on you," Jeremiah said, and then smiled. "That's the way they are."

And this is the way you are. You're right and they are wrong. That's it. Right? As long as you outnumber them you're in the right. You showed Frank. You sure showed him."

Jeremiah spread his hands out for silence to the boos that filled the bay. "So what is your understanding about niggers?"

Immediately I thought of Tell. "It's not about what color he is, it's about who he is. He's his own self, and is probably influenced by others around him, and sure he acts different among his own, but is that any different than white?" I spread my gaze to see the reaction. It was not good. But I could not stop. Brazenly, I marched on, the anger tightening my face, as if the heat wasn't doing it well enough.

"Never met a so-called nigger." My parents employed Negros at their cafeteria style restaurant, but I got along with them. In particular Mae, all 300 lbs. of her, who ran the kitchen like a general and the rest of us, including my parents, followed her orders in what she considered "her kitchen." My mother wanted me to work there washing pots and pans, when the regular man didn't show on the weekend. I did so knowing I had to follow Mae's orders. And adjustments were made as we grew accustomed to each other during one summer in 1950. I became a darn good pearl diver, she told my parents. I was proud of that assessment since I rarely scored high on my parent's goals of achievement.

In those days, away from the kitchen, my parents followed the white multitude and were closet racists. Colored people were invariably niggers when they did something my parents didn't like. When things went well, they were good people until the next time they did something unacceptable. I had my own feelings, based on my relationship with Mae. She was like a second mother during those summer days, me standing on a stack of metal trays as sweat pored out of me, as much from the temperature as the hot water my hands and arms swam in.

I told them most of that.

Silence followed for a few seconds.

"I can get along with anyone if they don't tell me how to think or act. Don't put your prejudices on me. Okay?"

"Nigger lover." It sounded like an indictment.

Anyone of them could have said it, but I didn't care. Although the thought of a bunk beating did occur to me as had Jopp. And I was a little anxious when I went in the shower later that evening, but nothing happened. And for reasons unknown, I slept like a baby.

Chapter Eight

It was our toughest inspection yet. A white glove, worn by the inspecting sergeant, hovered like a scimitar, ready to fall on someone's neck. What was at stake was a free weekend on base for those who passed. We stood at attention as the pending White Glove would seek out demerits, like a dusty window sill or an unclean brogan.

Sgt. Hardin, a staff sergeant, accompanied the Technical Sergeant, one grade higher, through his inspection of the barracks. The tech was enjoying himself as he strutted in a slow mosey down the center aisle of our first floor bay. We were braced at the foot of our bunks alongside our open footlockers as he strutted by. After one circuit up and down the aisle looking for something out of place, he pulled a pair of white gloves out of his pocket. In teasing ceremony he placed one finger at a time in one glove, then tugging it for overall snugness, then the other in agonizing slowness until he seemed satisfied. He turned his head to peek at Sgt. Hardin before the white gloves began in earnest to pounce on something unclean or out of order.

Sgt. Hardin had already made his own inspection. He knew from daily inspections whom his problem people were. He considered the failures as wayward, but didn't suggest to his platoon leaders that something be done to correct their bad habits. He talked to each in private. If a problem persisted, the squad leaders were notified. Rarely did someone fail another inspection.

As I stood rigidly, my confidence in being flawless in all prior inspections began leaking as I encountered a few smiles across from me. Not Mr. Happy smiles. I felt a nervousness, a shadow of paranoia sliding into unguarded spaces in my mind. I suddenly felt like the outsider I had become and I wondered if someone had sabotaged me. Even though we lived in an open bay, our personal areas were not open to others and not to be trespassed on, without permission. It was like a residential street, with only the street common ground, not the homes. Had I been vigilant or had someone slipped by unnoticed and tampered with my area? I couldn't get rid of the doubt.

After a tense 15 minutes, in which the white glove swiped many a surface and poked through a dozen footlockers, the inspector moved back to the center of the bay to make one last visual sweep before he stopped momentarily before Sgt. Hardin and said something not overheard before he went upstairs to the upper bay. My nervousness didn't lessen as renewed smiles spread out across our bay. I felt the conspiracy that would unveil itself when Sgt. Hardin returned. The heavy silence bore down on me as the minutes clicked by. Then Sgt. Hardin and White Glove returned. White Glove exited the barracks without a word. Sgt. Hardin looked at us impassively as he moved to the center of the bay, turned and looked at me. Then I knew. Somehow someone had gotten to me.

"Minus six upper, minus 4 lower," he said blandly.

What that meant was unclear. I kept my eyes on Sgt. Hardin, who no longer focused on me. He turned his eyes to my left and then looked downward. Sgt. Hardin then stepped up to Darren Wylie, who stiffened his brace. The sergeant's gaze moved to Wylie's footlocker. He peered inside, then bent down and pulled a paperback novel wedged between underwear and socks out and held it in his hand.

"Two demerits for this, and two demerits for the book itself "Catcher in the Rye."

That's it, you all passed. You did damn well. Enjoy your passes."

Our exultant roar was met with an echoing din from above that swept through the barracks. My nervousness ended as the roar became my roar and no one avoided my gaze as we sought out each other like a high school graduation celebration. I couldn't think of anything but what we had achieved working together. I knew it could be a new beginning, not letting our differences get in the way of Sgt. Hardin's goals. As much as I wanted it to be that way, I knew differently. This was not a cataclysmic event that changed the way people thought. It might influence some to accept others, including me, despite our differences. I had to hope for that small hope, even if it was wishful thinking.

I knew where I was going to go for my first liberty: to the bootblackers. We passed the shoe/boot shining facility daily on the way to mess. Airmen sporting their shiny brogans came out of the building with a new look on life, while others carried their glory in paper bags, shielding them from the elements or perhaps later to brag on the work they personally did. For my part, having someone do something that I was capable of wasn't to my liking. Others saw it different, perhaps because they couldn't duplicate the workmanship the Shiners worked into their shoes. I had seen the shine on shoes of those close to the end of their training. They were worn with a certain reverence for their beauty. I wanted to see who these craftsmen were and how they performed their mastery. Little Harry and Estaban asked to come along.

"I gotta see this. Someone said they put the shoes in a machine, and … " said Estaban.

"Ain't so," Little Harry interrupted. "I seen 'em when the door was open. Bunch a beaners. You'll see.

"Hey. Don't forget I'm half Mex. So watch yourself.

I gave Little Harry my evil eye.

His eyes said sorry, and I nodded.

If they can do it, so can we. It ain't like they're the only ones who can do it, Leeds said."

"You haven't seen anyone back in the barracks put on a shine like that, have you?" I retorted.

"Don't matter," he stated. "Maybe I'll put a little of my grease in the grain." He smiled at us, saying it was only okay for him to spout his Hispanic attributes.

We walked on, at a good clip, like we were marching. The sun gave us a mild reprieve from the cold, less now without a northerner. I turned my full attention to this new evolving world about me. It still intrigued me, the military way. In boot camp everything was clip-clip, always by the book. We were just numbers pouring out of the military funnel into a regimen of order and obedience. Now I tried to follow instincts to act freely, to be a tourist. We wore our green fatigue jackets our short-sleeved 505s for the first time, and I felt dressed up. I liked the tan look of the 505s, as much as I disliked the shabby green fatigues. I tried to separate myself from anything that was part of our everyday environment, but every rabbit trail ended up back on this military installation. As much as I tried to find another side to the base's personality, to make it more than I saw straight on, my imagination failed me. There was too much of the same thing to convert it into something that it was not. The only real difference was "us."

Would I look back at this experience and remember the base more than those I shared my experience with? The human element won hands down. Unfortunately, up to this point my judgment of my peers left an awful lot to be desired.

The bootblack facility was situated among a half dozen small buildings back to back apart from the base processing center. The stucco units, roughly 160 sq. ft., comprised a dry cleaner, a laudromat, and bakery on the near side, the bootblack, a barber, and a newsstand with hometown papers, candy and snacks on the other side. We had to pass by the bakery to get to the bootblack. Despite the mid-49s temperature, the front door was open, letting lose the aromas than beckoned our appetites.

Little Harry's insistence that we stop gave me the distinct impression this was his primary and perhaps only objective. Estaban was eager too, and I, having had a newspaper route bypass a bakery I often stopped in, wasn't disinclined. Little Harry was still in the bakery stowing up when I left with a couple of crullers, now eager to get to the bootblack.

As I turned the corner, I almost bumped into the giant TI that I had nicknamed "the Kisser," which paled in comparison to the uglier racial slurs of my flight brethren.

"Watch out there, young un," the Kisser said as he deftly slid by me, a large paper bag in one hand and a fat newspaper in the other.

Thrown off guard momentarily, I reacted impulsively, asking, "What paper have you got?"

It stopped him dead in his tracks. He pivoted effortlessly and thrust his beady eyed face toward me, his eyes as intent as Little Harry's in the bakery.

"What did you say?"

I guess he was incredulous that I had spoken to him, but he was not angry. "I asked what paper you've got?"

"Well, let me see," he said, tucking the paper bag between his chin and chest. He turned the paper toward me and let me see that it was The New York Times.

I didn't need to look at the masthead to know the look of The Times. I nodded while surreptitiously eyeing the brown bag hanging from his throat. My first impulse was that they could be hiding shined shoes? My first thought was that he was too lazy to shine his own shoes. My considered judgment was that my prejudice was annoying me. Maybe it had nothing to do with laziness or excessive pride, but expediency or maybe they were being resoled. Why was I doing this? The Kisser was a cartoon character, a fabrication of my imagination. But I was also curious and that, of course, inevitably would lead me to trouble.

For his part, he did not simply dismiss me, and thereby keep me from another undoing. He leaned forward and I thought for a fraction that he was going to plant one on me. Keeping his chin snugly on the paper bag, his big head stayed low and nimbly he folded back one section and announced what section it was. I didn't know what to say or do, so I paid strict attention to the paper. He went through the entire paper, describing each section, then said: "Are you okay with this purchase of mine?"

I heard his voice -- my eyes still on the paper – which hadn't hardened but hinted at indignation. I knew it was none of my business, but I wasn't fazed by any sense of impropriety. It was just my curiosity, even though I was prepared to be castigated for speaking out of turn if it came to that.

Again, he surprised me. In a voice as smooth as his step, he asked, "Are you familiar with The Times?"

I guess it was the word "familiar" that caught my attention, sticking in my mind and turning it over like an engine. My mind revved up and settled on the incongruity of his speech. This wasn't a word that an uneducated lout uses. It had not jumped out at me at first because I was caught off guard, but now I realized the difference. Either the Kisser had a twin brother, or he was posing as an illiterate. I sensed that it was an act. This was the real person and I had the sense of him being "cultured," given the Times in his hand. We had all been taken in by what seemed to be natural behavior for the hideous black noncom. As my mind whirled trying to fit every iota of information I had of him, I realized he was looking at me with anticipation of my answer. A response was asked. I tried to focus on one as my mind seemed somewhere else. I could not think of how to respond. What came out was a natural blurt.

"I was a paperboy as a kid. I do the crosswords, like my dad. I know papers. Then added, thoughtlessly, "I was curious."

"Don't you remember being told in childhood that curiosity killed the cat. For some reason I feel you have very few lives remaining. Are you a chronic troublemaker?" By now he was speaking in his intimidating voice, soft but deadly.

"No, sir, I mean, no sergeant." I came to attention.

"What do you have in your hand?

"Crullers, sergeant."

"You are at attention," he barked. Which meant

why are you holding those crullers while at attention?

I should have stooped to put them down on the pavement, but his eye contact unnerved me. Instead I dropped them.

The sergeant continued to eye me sternly. I felt his intimidation weakening me and it was a matter of seconds before I broke eye contact. But then I felt something below the surface of that glowering countenance -- the hint of an emerging smile. He was enjoying this, my anticipated discomfort, but something else was going on and I could feel a stupid smile coming on in reply.

"Have a nice day," he said abruptly, half turned and moved off silently.

But in that half turn I caught the emerging smile, saw his cheek fill out in his escape from me. Would that smile have meant a human gesture passed between us, that I was not merely a contemptible recruit unworthy of a simple human gesture? I stood there trying to fully understand what had just happened between us, when Estaban sidled up to me.

"Ya oughta see Harry. He's got enough donuts for the whole bay. Kid's got a real sweet tooth."

I bent to pick up my crullers.

"What happened?"

"Wasn't watching where I was going and bumped into a guy. They fell."

"They still good?" he asked, turning them over in my hand. "No dirt."

"Heck, yeah. Dirt don't bother me."

Silently we waited for Little Harry. The sun was warming us when the winds died and I felt excited that something had happened to me that didn't end badly. Enthusiasm warmed me and I was eager to see the shiners. Little Harry met my deadline and the three of us turned the corner to the bootblack.

A single row of four steel chairs on a riser were occupied and attended my four Mexicans, who worked in a flurry. The action, as well as the sounds, was mesmerizing. One lean young man with a thick shock of black hair grabbed my attention by the snapping of a fleece polishing cloth before and after it was worked over one brogan, then the other. The snap crackled the air in a "pop." He was as much a Showman as a shoe shiner. When he finished, he tapped the top of the brogans with the tips of his fingers, stepped back and pivoted while sweeping his hand in a bow. Like a toreador to a passing bull. The customer, an airman second class, fished out his payment in dollars and handed them to the young man as he moved off the stand.

"Muchos gracias," the Showman said with a wide

smile.

In a flicker a new customer was atop the stand.

We watched the other shiners finish off their customers unceremoniously and collect their payment. The turnover was quick, the shiners hustling through a dozen airmen in less than a half hour.

"You want boots?" the Showman said to me, looking down at my brogans.

"No. But they do," I said motioning to Little Harry and Estaban.

"No. You need boots," he said urgently, pointing at my brogans with a serious look.

I replied that they were already "shiny."

"No. Not good. Make better," he said with a wide smile."

I didn't budge.

"Okay, GI," he said, then beckoned to Little Harry without missing a beat.

Handing his donuts over to me, Little Harry bounded up to the chair and once settled in, asked for his donuts.

Simultaneously, the Showman spoke a flurry of words that brought laughter from his co-workers.

When one of the shiners made a quick sidelong peek at me, I knew the comments were about me, not Little Harry. I turned toward Estaban, for a translation. He merely smiled, conceding nothing. Something had transpired between the Showman and Estaban. I knew him well enough to know he would only tell me later if he was so inclined. Whatever was transpired was personal. But I wanted to be personal in response. Perhaps a polite GET FUCKED, ASSHOLE.

Meanwhile I watched the Showman work on Little Harry's brogans. "Snap. Snap. Snap" Every move was a flourish. He knew how to work the crowd I was no longer part of, piqued by his comments, whatever their content.

In one of his flourishes, he turned sideways and glanced at me again. Instantly another comment brought more laughter. I could feel the irritation rising like a rash but didn't know what to say or do.

Estaban, eyeing his compadre, came to my rescue. "Tell him, 'Beso me culo."

"What's that mean?"

"Don't worry. He knows."

So I said it.

Showman's co-workers burst into louder laughter than they had given me. Apparently I had hit a nerve as the Showman bristled and made a louder snap and spat something back at them. Dead silence followed. No more snaps. Not a mumble.

"Let's go," whispered Estaban, tugging my arm. He beckoned Little Harry with an urgent finger. Little Harry was finishing up his last donut and was reluctant to get up. Estaban was insistent with a wave of his hand. Little Harry fumbled with his wallet and finally extracted some bills as the silence stretched tighter. Then Little Harry moved to get down. The Showman didn't budge, blocking him. Suddenly the little room seemed to shrink as the tension zoomed in on us.

Little Harry began to realized we were alone with him being blocked in. His fear became ours. Then Estaban thrust out his hand and nudged the Showman, who stood up with a dark scowl on his face. Everyone knew that look. And the intent. Little Harry tossed three bills at the Showman and scurried off the chair and past us as we backed out, Estaban eyeing the Showman, who scurried to collect his payment. Little Harry slammed the door as we cleared it.

"Why is it you can't stay out of trouble?" spat Estaban. "You never know what them beaners will do. They all carry knives and know how to use them." He grinned.

"From Day One you've stuck your nose where it doesn't belong. And what do you have to show for it?

That asshole and this asshole. Boy, you are never going to get anywhere with that attitude." Estaban's grin was wider than ever.

Chapter Nine

Sgt. Hardin was not in a good mood as dawn broke and a distant siren was sounded, squealing like an angry pig. I knew that sound but it didn't connect down here in Texas. The skies were pewter and the clouds roiled in anticipation of something ominous, but it was chow time, so those of us going to morning mess were moving outside and assembling in formation, anxious to get going. Normally talk was minimal and in low tones since Sgt. Hardin forbade "chatter," which in his bad days meant even coughing. Since he had the hang dog look of a hangover even though he didn't drink to excess, I surmised that he wasn't a morning person. Some days he was downright surly and kept us on edge until his moodiness seemingly changed with the weather. When it cleared up, so did he. The early morning buzz was what we expected of him as the gray skies fumed and fussed above us. We were not startled when he burst out of the barracks, his hands settling on his hips as he glowered at us from our step porch.

"And just where the hell do you think you are going?"

We were dumbstruck. I was sure others knew we had nothing scheduled for the morning. In the afternoon we were set for the rifle range, but the morning was free except for daily cleanup. Jeremiah looked at me quizzically, but got nothing.

"I'm waiting for an answer," Sgt. Hardin said impatiently.

"Chow, sergeant," Bo offered a bit sheepishly.

"Let me get this straight. If you were back home in Hog Hollow and you walked out on your front porch, that is if you had a front porch, and looked up in the sky and saw that ...," he said pointing upward, "would you ignore it and go feed the pigs?"

Bo was baffled. He looked at Jeremiah for help, but it wasn't forthcoming. "Well, I don't rightly know" he hedged. "We don't have pigs."

A few titters couldn't be helped.

"Golly gee, I musta overstepped myself. Let me simplify myself. Have you never seen the makings of a tornado alongside the porch? What did you think that siren was for?

"Hurry up and git your asses inside," Sgt. Hardin blared. "Move it, move it."

We did, scrambling by him as he held the door open. I avoided eye contact, feeling remiss for something. After the main throng passed him by, he slammed the screen door and muttered "idiots."

Chow suddenly had become a necessity and chow calls were yelled as we exited and reassembled in formation. Sgt. Hardin came out but decided otherwise. He yelled to Jeremiah to take us to chow and went back inside.

We were excited as we began marching. We had become good marchers, not from learning the fundamentals of drill, but because of Jeremiah's ribald cadences. They took us away from what we were doing as an exercise and placed us in a relaxing atmosphere.

I recalled how slow to learn we had been under Sgt. Hardin's tutelage at drill until we heard our first relaxing cadence. It came from an unexpected source.

We were at the squadron's drill pad, an asphalt expanse that allowed as many as four flights at once, but usually only one or two were on the pad at the same time. We were there one sunny morning, sweating in our fatigues, trying to execute a left turn en masse. We were failing miserably, unable to twist into it when a cadence drill broke the heavy air. It was a lively cadence we had heard before, but like any song how the singer sang it made the difference. We were marching away from the oncoming flight, so we couldn't see who it was, but the sound stimulated us. Sgt. Hardin's cadence counts were straight forwardly ordinary, basic grunts and flavorless.

We had asked for more, but Sgt. Hardin wasn't forthcoming. He was a hard one to change.

Probably because of our lack of execution on the left turn and Sgt. Hardin's impatience, he brought us to a halt. We stirred in anticipation of seeing who was approaching, but the sergeant wasn't having any of it.

"You're at attention, eyes straight ahead," he barked.

It was agonizing not being able to see the approaching flight behind us. The tantalizing sounds had engulfed us. Now the unseen flight was rhythmically responding. You could hear their enjoyment, the pleasure it gave them to vocally reply, to be a chorus. Their brogans beat synchronously in what sounded like an effortless pattern.

As I listened, my sweat evaporated in a wave of coolness brought by some mental stimulation. I could feel a difference surging though me. I wanted so much for us to be together like that, executing like a metronome, effortlessly, uninhibited by prejudice or discord. I had to look.

"Eyes straight," Sgt. Hardin bellowed as if reading my/our minds.

I went rigid, the spell broken, sweat assuming its posture on my warm skin.

Sgt. Hardin's eyes, I could see, remained on us

unflinchingly. He was paying no attention to anyone but us as he knew we were thinking only of the group behind us. The sounds of the brogans hitting pavement were weakening. For some reason the flight was moving on. The air was oppressive as the sounds faded. Rivulets of sweat tickled my neck. I felt defeated.

The last sounds heard were a mumbling rhythm, a reminder of cadence that held together the beat of their brogans.

We remained stiff at attention longer than I expected. I had the feeling we were being punished, not for our inept left turn, but for craving what we heard and suspecting we would never get there.

That episode was singly the most talked about drilling event during our training. We never heard that sound again. It was as if it or they didn't exist. They were a figment of our imagination during a difficult time.

Jeremiah was our only reprieve, accepted as a worthy imitation, as we eased our way to the mess hall. The bounce I got out of it also uplifted others. We eased along like a well-oiled machine, effortlessly flowing with the rhythm of his voice and our imagination.

"I got a girl," -- .he began in a sing-song manner, his voice upbeat and our bodies limbering up with anticipation, -- "from Old Kantuck"

It warmed us that we were flaunting the rules of

good conduct with Jeremiah's suggestive rhythms.

"Smiles at me when she wants to HUT, two three, four."

It put us in an idyllic mood, particularly if you had seen that picture of Jeremiah's wife, and I was sure he made sure everyone saw it. She personified the single most used word in our world. Fuck.

But there was the other kind of "fuck," the one that preceded something we'd rather not be doing, including cleaning the barracks, which preceded inspections, which led to gigs, which led to be unfit for military life and ouster from the service. That was the worst, but sounded as bad because of the grousing. I was convinced that a lot of the worst grousers were those who were inactive as civilians, and now forced into activity complained ad nauseum. For my part, they were those I secretly put on the worst barrack duty, hoping it would change their attitudes. I rarely saw any change, so they remained there without replacement. If they ever found out I'd be in the shits.

The other duties that drew grousing were among my favorites, KP (kitchen patrol) and PT (physical training). KP was a one time only duty, for the whole flight, unless circumstances required a severe punishment. KP had us cleaning up the mess and washing dishes for split six hour shifts, six a.m. to 2 p.m. and 2 p.m. to 8 p.m.

PT, to my thinking, was an absolute necessity, and

hence a target for grousing. Many recruits were really out of shape and needed to be much more fit, not combat ready like the other military services. For my part, scraping food off plates and washing dishes in hot water was natural for me, and getting exercise doing side straddle hops and push ups, etc. was the fitness I needed to round off my three squares a day stuffing anything and everything in my stomach. I could feel a strength building on my growing body.

Therein lies an experience I will never forget. I reveled in the need of exercise to tone up. It was in the second week, during a slightly warm spell. If the weather was inclement or harshly cold, PT took place in an empty aircraft hanger, otherwise it was held outdoors within the parade grounds, The frosty north wind was swirling elsewhere, the sky clear and crispy blue. As we approached the parade grounds, which was spread a half mile northward like a high school football field with square concrete corners, another flight was exercising at the other end, their arms and legs winging in and out as if trying to propel them skyward.

In the middle of an expanse in the south end was a cross barred wooden platform standing six feet high with someone on top and wearing the same outfit as ourselves, a white tee shirt and pinkish gym shorts. Sgt. Hardin marched us up close to the platform as a gangly guy watched. Bring us to a halt, Sgt. Hardin walked away, toward the platform.

Immediately, the physical training instructor yelled for us to stand at ease. We responded. He then instructed us to spread out according to his instruction. Once spread, he explained in a loud commanding voice to follow his movements after he showed us how to do the exercise, a side straddle hop. He made the same movements as the group I saw coming to the field. It was simple enough. He stopped, then instructed us to follow those moves. We followed his brisk pace, but quickly some failed and their failure threw off the timing of many others behind and in view of them.

"Halt," he barked.

We settled down, but laughter broke out.

Quickly he responded. "Attention."

We jumped to attention, except for a few, perhaps still laughing.

He repeated his order, staring at those to my right. Then he turned to Sgt. Hardin, standing aside the platform smoking a cigarette, and spoke to him. The sergeant nodded.

The instructor pointed toward us and yelled, "You, you, you." His finger pinpointed the offenders as his face tightened. Then satisfied with his choices, he ordered them to advance to him. While they moved, he turned his attention toward us.

"These three did not follow an order and will be running a lap for their disobedience. If they stop at any time before finishing, they will continue until I am satisfied. Anyone failing to follow my orders will do the same. Do you understand?"

What to say was misunderstood. We didn't know his rank. Responses were awkward or mumbled.

"I am your instructor. Reply accordingly." His voice and countenance was matter of fact. He was back in control.

"Yes, instructor," we replied

To the threesome he waved his hand toward the concrete pad and ordered them to begin running.

They stumbled off, scattering to different locations, which brought titters.

"I'm surrounded by assholes and idiots," the instructor muttered.

We continued our exercises without interruption. The runners were plodding, barely making a stride when they returned. The instructor spoke to Sgt. Hardin, who twirled a finger in the air.

"While we are enjoying an extracurricular activity, you three will be running another lap. Is that clear? Running. Not walking, not talking, not even enjoying yourselves. Move out!

He turned to us. "Attention." He eyed us balefully. "Fall out."

Quickly he pointed toward an oblong wooden box. "The equipment is there." Then he jumped down and began walking toward the box.

I started there too, when I saw Sgt. Hardin put his arm out. The instructor stopped and they spoke. I turned away.

The box was emptied of two footballs, a couple softballs, a bat and a large pair of boxing gloves. Everything except the gloves was taken and groups assembled and moved off. I stood alone, mulling over what I would do when Sgt. Hardin walked up to me.

"Did I hear someone call you "Scrap?" he said easy like. "Isn't that a boxing term?"

"Could mean a lot of things, but yeah, maybe a little boxing wouldn't hurt me." I was thinking that since I felt I excelled at the first two why not get some slicks in with the 15 ounce gloves. There was a certain appeal not yet defined.

Impulse, you murderer. Without thinking I blurted, "Anyone want to box?"

In an instant, a half dozen guys answered and turned back toward us. How so many acted so quickly to say "yes" to my offer should have been a clue to me, but there it was. My challenge, their response.

Sgt. Hardin volunteered to referee since the instructor had something he had to leave for. It surprised me, though, when he declared three one round matches would be held that afternoon, but took down names for subsequent exhibitions. Even before I put my gloves on the word was spread and drew a lot of attention. Too much attention. Bells started going off in my mind.

"What the fuck you doing?" questioned Estaban.

Before I could respond, Harry encouraged me. "That fucker's slower than dirt."

What that meant escaped me. But I had one backer.

Harry, who later I felt had enjoyed the taste of blood, acted as my second, massaging my arms and neck and moved adroitly explaining what I should do.

Estaban just shook his head as if I deserved my fate.

After my first bout, more than bells rang. An unforeseen roundhouse right by one of the duty roster regulars decked me a mid cheers. Eventually I learned to keep my left shoulder up and tucked in to ward off cousins of that devastating blow. It took me a while to figure out a workable offense. I survived nonetheless, arm weary and spent, but not really hurt any in the next two bouts.

Later that night, still the talk of the upper floor and

fresh from a long, hot shower my bunkie kept smiling at me while shaking his head. Finally, I had had enough.

"What the fuck's up with you anyhow."

"Well, you saved my ass, I guess it's time to ..., he started.

"Hey, you don't owe me anything. What I did I'd have done for anyone. It's not ...

Just fucking listen. "I know you're making up the duty roster. And guess ..."

"What do you mean?" I interjected.

"And they do too," Estaban said, shaking his head.

"How? Who?" I was flabbergasted

"By now, everyone, top and bottom." Estaban shook his head again, but slower and pathetically.

I believed him. It wasn't a matter of how as much as whom. Candidate No. 1 had to be Jeremiah, but I couldn't figure out his motive.

Estaban, who didn't fail to astonish me with his logic and more so, his instincts, caused me to pause and not put my brain to a task beyond my ken. I turned my mind away and thought of something different, trying to focus on it completely. How many dishes could I clean in a minute? I could feel the hot water soothe my hands as I dipped a plate in hot water, swirled the washrag in my hands across the face of the plate and set it aside. I followed that procedure as I counted out sixty seconds.

Mae asked how many.

"Fourteen, I said."

"Don't you drop any of my dishes, now

I registered the look on her smiling brown, cherubic face. It was loving. As it faded and I decided to try for 15 plates, my thought diffused and up came another face.

Sgt. Hardin's. He had motive and as I tried to recreate a scene in my mind at the PT field, the thought occurred that he was in total control with the instructor leaving. I made a little grimace: payback.

"You figured it out?" Estaban asked.

"The sergeant."

"Yep. I watched him in that first bout. He was telegraphing his own punches to that fuckup.

Surprisingly I wasn't angry or bitter.

"But what if I had refused to box?"

"What could you do if you were challenged? You think of that? He sucked you in, maybe even sneaking in the notion that you'd be labeled a coward. I wasn't there then.

"No, I don't think he'd do that. You know, it was my own idea." I shook my head, feeling a bit stupid. I guess there was a learning curve that was swerving beyond my grasp. I let it go, putting it down to mistakes made by immaturity. I had to figure out if I was going to confront him with it. It was something to think about.

In the intervening weeks, we collectively did well at the rifle range, with no one shooting anyone, were passable at the gas chamber, and completed the obstacle course with relatively few injuries. We got by, which seemed to satisfy Sgt. Hardin, and we gained more confidence in doing things right quicker. We were past the point of washing out. We had survived and looked forward to the end of basic training. We were suddenly short timers, with just a week to go.

Chapter Ten

I was excited and forlorn. Our orders were in. We were to find out that afternoon what we were going to be trained for after basic training. My options were wide spread because I had scored well on the entrance exam at the induction center. Others had signed up specifically for a single duty, but were nonetheless excited because a two week leave followed the end of basic. It was that excitement that got me up. And down.

A reluctance had evolved as separation from these guys would occur within the week. Despite our differences, we had developed a level of tolerance of each other because of our shared experiences. I ended up having only six additional boxing matches, the last two of which I won, not surprisingly from my own roundhouse right. That ended all contentions. I was no longer an easy standing target. And eruptions didn't flare as they had earlier. Yet I knew a spark remained where a searing fire once scorched. What had earlier been open enmity now showed itself as gallows humor. We laughed at things we had been ready to go to battle over.

The joke developed that anyone who was bound for the Motor Pool was brain dead. The laughter was contagious and eased any hard feelings, or so it seemed. I stood off on the sidelines, as I was prone to do, and observed.

"What do think you're going to do, Jon?" asked Jeremiah, ringmaster to our parade of fools.

"No idea. Air traffic controller, meteorologist, linguist and a couple more were on the qualification listing."

"Well, I guess I shouldn't be surprised," said Jeremiah, and smiled in what seemed to be his farewell. He turned away and asked another the same question.

"Knock, knock," said the voice of Sgt. Hardin, who beckoned me when I turned with an index finger.

I followed him into his neat, Spartan room. Other than a bed, a desk and chair, there was nothing of personal value. Not a picture. Or a book. Or a lamp. I was confused.

He closed the door after I followed him in. Sgt. Hardin and I rarely spoke, particularly because of our duty roster arrangement, and then when he blew my cover I felt betrayed. I added some resentment from the boxing episode, but considering I learned from it, I wasn't that annoyed. From where I stood, it was almost a wash, except for my doubts that I could trust what he said.

"Got a request from command," he said as he swiveled into a chair. "I need a trainee to represent the squadron for a base recognition award. Have one every six months. I'd like your input." He eyed me with amusement slowly spreading across his face.

"Why me?" I hesitated, trying to get a feel of what was going on. My instincts gave me nothing. Unable to think of anything in particular, I spoke too quickly.

"Ask your squad leaders." My comment bordered on contempt, which could get me in big trouble, but some resentment had to be understood. Again a wash, hoped. Still I couldn't figure out what he was doing. "This is a joke?" I dared say.

A spreading smile came to his face. "Nope. Straight dope."

"This is not a joke?"

"You're not intimidated by me, are you?"

What he was leading up to I didn't know, but I had a funny feeling I would soon find out.

"I've learned a lot from you, sergeant, and … "

"Does anyone in the flight come to mind as someone who best represents us?"

I had to think about it. Was there a standout? As I

pondered this, Sgt. Hardin stretched his upper body and arms. My attention turned to him. He was a handsome man, of middle age, short dark hair with a part, and a lean, compact frame. His long sleeved uniform always pressed. I had the feeling he was neat, whatever clothing he wore. I wondered about his personal life.

"I can tell you are wondering what I am getting at, rather than thinking about what I asked. That's only natural, I guess, your sergeant asking you to help him out."

Then he did something that totally threw me off. He began rolling up his sleeves, neatly, precisely, overlapping the creases, like he was getting ready to get dirty. He smiled and spoke again.

My attention was riveted to him.

"You remember our first meeting. Of course. Everyone in the flight remembers it. You singled yourself out standing up for someone you didn't know. Both of you should have been tossed out, like that," he said, snapping his fingers. "But you caught me off guard. Totally.

"I was impressed, or should I say you made an impression." He seemed to settle in, getting more comfortable, crossing his legs and easing back in his chair. Then suddenly he sprang forward in his chair and looked me squarely in the eyes. "No. I was impressed." That said, he eased back and began to mull over what he was going to say.

The silence didn't bother me, but the quiet in the barracks had me wondering what was going on.

"We cannot be anyone other than your drill instructors. You understand that. We drill you until your first nature is to follow orders. Everything is a drill to execute an order. We live by order and drill."

He paused, I suspect, to let that sink in. I did not break into the silence, wanting to hear all of what he had to say without commenting. I understood the order and drill mentality. I waited out his breaks in conversation.

"I'm from Minnesota."

There it was. I was dumbfounded. Utterly stunned. It was a personal comment that changed our relationship. He was in uncharted waters, I could sense, but wasn't ill at ease.

"We have our lives off-base. We don't bring that life here. This is a job that needs to be done and I do my job well. For your part, you have done your job well. You have made my job easier, but easy is not what this job is about. It is about performance. You have performed well all-around, so I am making you the squadron's best trainee."

He held up his hands to keep me from interrupting. "It is military knowledge, best known to those with

ROTC background, so you will probably lose.

"On the other hand, your orders have not come in. The training school you will be attending, in Syracuse, New York, will not take in another class for at least seven more weeks." Then he said something like "horror show."

My countenance didn't display recognition, so he continued.

"You don't yet speak Russian, but you will. Syracuse, like Monterey, California and Indiana University, is where Russian language training takes place. So I suspect you will be trained as a Russian translator. That's pretty impressive."

I remembered the language fluency test I got among other tests at induction, but I didn't recall any specific language was mentioned. Russia. Our Cold War adversary. I was intrigued.

"It is not a difficult language. My folks up in Minnesota speak it a little because of their neighbors. We all learned a little bit of everything. We had Poles, Finns, Rooskies, the lot. You will do well. But until then you will have temporary duty in the squadron and be assistance to a DI.

I was staying here. I was thrilled. Sgt. Hardin wanted me to help him out.

"Have you ever heard of the name Cletus Huckaby?"

Cletus Huckaby. I was stunned. Anyone from Detroit who was a sports fan knew that name, but it had nothing to do with the Air Force. "Yah. Sure," I mumbled.

"Being from up north, chances are you might if you know sports. He played … "

"Football. With Detroit. Offensive line. But what …?"

Sgt. Hardin smiled. "He played a couple of good years, but got hurt."

"I know. He was big, the biggest guard in the league. He was bigger than Les Bingaman. He opened holes in the defense I could've gone through untouched." I could talk for hours about Detroit sports. "He hurt his leg or ankle. Those were the weak points. We were one of the best teams because of him, and Alex Karras, and Joe Schmidt."

"He had some leg problems, but it was his head. Coulda been a concussion. He doesn't talk about it. He doesn't think the way you and I do anyhow. You'll see."

I was confused. What did Huckaby have to do with me.

Sgt. Hardin could see I hadn't made the connection yet. "Let me help you out. Cletus is a TI, been one for six years here in the 96th. You're staying with him until that language school of yours is ready for you."

"I thought I was staying here." My disappointment was obvious.

"I recommended you, but he knew you already. He asked for you."

"But, but, why did you recommend me?"

"I know you can give him what he needs."

Now I was edging toward a mistake because I was not getting what I wanted. I felt a discomfort settling in on me. I hesitated to say anything while my silent boil was rising. I could feel that I was going too far, stepping too close to that well-known edge between reason and anger. Without knowing why, reason pulled me back, but anger was in my voice. "What does he need?"

Sgt. Hardin didn't change posture or flare back at me. In a composed manner he told me. "He needs someone like you to give him time alone."

Before I could blurt out something in response he put a finger to his lips. I waited momentarily, abiding his gesture. Before I could spill out my undoing, he spoke.

"I know I can trust you not to say anything. He gets bad headaches. They call them migraines."

My anger dissipated as quickly as it had risen and I

felt the relief. For a long time, my mother suffered from migraines. They were treated like an illness. She took medication that rarely seemed to work. It affected the family, our daily life style. We had our blinds closed throughout the day to keep the sunlight out; we rarely raised our voices. My father and I did the shopping because Mom was virtually a shut-in. Then one day the headaches disappeared. It was a life changer.

"Because of his head injury?"

"They got a name for it, but I forgot. He won't go for help. I've tried. And besides, he's not who you think he is. I know the name you have for him. He has been called many things worse."

Suddenly the Kisser's face loomed in my mind, like a nasty black cloud ready to unload a torrent of venom. Then it disappeared as quickly and the other side of him surfaced. I could empathize with his suffering. Yet I was disconcerted over my feelings and it must have showed.

"You have no idea who he is or what he is capable of, so don't sit there thinking you know him. You have to give him a chance to show himself." He paused.

"I have. I mean he has." I recounted my encounter with him. As I talked, Sgt. Hardin relaxed.

"Now you know, and yes, that's what he is, but even knowing that doesn't explain everything. "It's not easy holding back all the time. It's no easier letting someone in. That's dangerous in many ways.

"It's just that I wanted to stay here."

"For my part, I'd like you to stay here, too. But you will help Cletus a lot better than you would me. Besides, once you really know the man, you will never forget him.

He could have said "enough said," as he was prone to, but his pronouncement that I would never forget him held its own punctual finality. I thought immediately of the New York Times episode. It occurred to me that maybe that was how he came to recognize me, but I couldn't figure how he connected me to Sgt. Hardin. Curiosity made me respond.

"So how does he know about me?"

"You'll have to ask him -- if you dare." A big challenging smile emerged on his handsome face.

I guess he knew I would have to ask him, so I smiled back. It felt great to be there doing what we were doing like real people, just talking. It was the first time in basic that I felt real enjoyment. Enough said.

Chapter Eleven

As I approached the base headquarters, I tried to squeeze off my nervousness. I was not prepared for the base recognition award contest. Sgt. Hardin gave me no clue as to its content, but told me my appearance was just as important as the test. My dress shoes shined as did all the brass buttons on my dress blues blouse. I had left the barracks with the notion that I looked the part, clean and sparkling. I comforted myself with my clipboard mentality of going ahead in a professional manner and everything would work out for itself. After all, I wasn't a dummy.

"I'm here to represent the 96th in the base recognition award contest," I said to the desk sergeant, who was straightening his desk.

He continued his straightening, hesitated, glanced up at me as if I had interrupted a vital task, then stoically pointed to his left.

My eyes followed to a cubicle with four schoolhouse chairs, all unoccupied. I looked back at the sergeant, who had gone back to straightening his desk. He was ignoring me. I cleared my throat.

"What is it?"

"I was told …" I began, when he glowered at me. I stopped in mid-sentence.

"Go over there and take the test," he said irritably.

I was confused, having been told that everyone would be taking the test at the same time. "There's no one else there, and I was told …"

"Are you stupid or what?"

"I was told …"

"The test is over there," he said condescendingly. "You have 30 minutes to finish. When I ring this bell, stop, and then bring back your test sheet. Have you got that?"

I admit to being flustered, but went to the cubicle chastised for what, I didn't know. Before I sat down I looked about for witnesses to the sergeant's behavior toward me. No one was in sight. I felt like a condemned prisoner. The test was no reprieve.

Sgt. Hardin was right about the base recognition award. I didn't stand a chance. There were 20 fill-in-the-blank questions. Many of them were numbers I had to identify. I figured 13 represented the 13 original states, but had no idea the number of soldiers in a various sized group. I struggled through it like it was trigonometry, my worst class in high school. Finally I finished, but the stress still held me uncomfortably. I wanted to feel better about my effort, to get some relief so I decided to go over it again and maybe inspiration might pull out some better answers. To no avail, I got up sluggishly with a test sheet that felt like an anvil. I had only to get by the desk sergeant who, with head down, was now shuffling papers. As I came to his desk, he abruptly thrust up a hand to take my test sheet.

He made a quick look at it, one in which I figured he wanted to make sure I filled the heading out correctly.

"Not even close," said the sergeant, head still down.

His brusqueness stung me. I stood there numbed with inadequacy and unable to move.

"Not to worry, bub," said the sergeant, who was gazing up at me now. "The one oh first got 'em all." The sergeant wore a sneering self-satisfied smile.

To my relief, only Sgt. Hardin was interested in my return.

"You were right," I said apologetically to the sergeant, who was smoking a cigarette at the front entrance of our barracks.

"Your sergeant is always right, remember?"

"Even the desk sergeant gave me a rough time," I said as I sat down along side him.

"No doubt. Did he tell you the one-oh-first won?"

"How'd you know that?"

Sgt. Hardin gazed up at the blue sky, barely a cloud in sight, and took another drag on his dwindling smoke. He turned to me, looking me squarely in the eye, smiled, and turned back to reflect on a cloudless sky.

I waited impatiently, looking upward too. There were no answers there, but I figured I had to wait him out. My thoughts drifted in the swirling wind.

"It's a small world here," he said without preamble.

"When did you find out, sir?"

Sgt. Hardin quickly turned to me, his countenance hard.

Somehow I had gaffed. I thought again what I had said, but came up empty. Was I too inquisitive or overstepping my position? I looked at his hardened eyes. It scared me how quickly he changed.

Then he saw something in me that softened him. It was a small, wry smile that surfaced.

"Sir?" It was almost a whisper floating on the wind. In an instant I came to realize what the word was I had said but it wasn't inappropriate. I meant it out of respect, and again, he picked up on it.

"I appreciate it, considering." The small, wry smile stayed intact.

"I didn't mean any disrespect ... sergeant, I just ..."

"Not to worry. But don't go around loose with others. As I said, it's a small world, and not everyone is," he said, pausing. "Well, never mind." And then he chuckled. "I haven't talked this much in a coon's age." Now he was staring at the cloudless sky. Smiling to himself occasionally. Thinking.

I took it as time to leave him to his solitary thoughts. I rose, pulling myself up with the handrail, but my twisted hand slipped and I lost my balance. I began to fall backwards.

Sgt. Hardin came out of his reverie and quickly reached out to catch me. I fell awkwardly in his taut arms but bumped my head on the top step. It hurt, but my embarrassment kept me from voicing it. His strong arms released me.

I turned to him, catching a humorous grin splayed across his handsome face.

He began to slowly shake his head. "I don't know how you do it. You can't keep your balance and they make you a Physical Training Instructor."

"What?"

"Yeah. Can you believe it?

"A PTI? They're letting me PT?" It was incredulous. Of all the duties, PT was one of the best. I was ecstatic.

"You'll probably fall off the platform and break your neck first time out."

"Really. I can't believe it." I was overjoyed. "When do I start?"

"Monday. And, Breckinridge, Sgt. Huckaby, is expecting you tomorrow around 1700. Don't be late. Get all your stuff together. I don't imagine you'll have many goodbyes to say. Just make sure you're on time."

A PTI. I couldn't get over it. I felt the physical strength which had developed over the past six weeks. I had gained more than 25 pounds and an inch in height. I was by far in the best physical condition of my life. And now a PTI. As I left Sgt. Hardin on the front steps, I was still on cloud nine. I strutted to my bunk, oblivious to others.

As I was changing to fatigues from my dress blues, I could feel the eyes on me. But no one approached and I was not disappointed. My being chosen as the squadron's representative didn't sit well with some. Although I had no choice in the matter, it looked like I considered myself better than them. I had been congratulated by just three, Estban, Little Harry, and Jeremiah, who did it discreetly.

Changed into my fatigues, I plopped down on my made bunk, which had already been inspected while I was out for the base recognition test. Lying down seemed to keep my mind open and I wanted to savor the thought of being a PTI. In the midst of seeing myself on the platform high above everyone else, gazing at the throng before me, Little Harry kicked the metal side of my bunk. I recognized the kick, which was Little Harry's way of saying hello.

"Hey, Harry." Little Harry wasn't little anymore. With the three squares a day and the donut shop, he had put on at least 20 pounds and muscled up. And his face cleared up of the acne that kept him in bondage as a mid-teen. And more important, he was maturing. No longer was he the little kid on the block. He took on an aggressive pose to some, an even keel to others, including me.

"So, how'd it go?"

For my part, I didn't let him just wing it at me. "You talkin' to me?"

"Ya-uh."

I knew how soft Little Harry's underbelly was and where to jab my fingers, if necessary. The verbal jabbing was usually enough. "As a Base Recognition Award candidate, I don't talk to just anyone, especially those who go around kicking their bunks."

"C'mon, Jon," he said, weakening.

"I don't think so, Harry," I said snobbishly.

"Tell me." It was his one and only last, best effort.

"Nope, candidates don't have to talk to riff-raff."

"J-o-o-o-n, c'mon"

"If you swear to keep it between us."

"Sure. So how'd you do?"

I beckoned him with my index finger to come closer. He squatted alongside the bunk. "I died with my boots on."

"What happened?'

"My blood was all over the test sheet."

"Really? You fucked up."

"No, I didn't fuck up as you crudely put it. I just didn't, well, know what they could possibly ask, so I decided to wing it. That's how I fucked up."

Harry just smiled, as if in his glory.

"Don't be so happy, you asshole."

That did it. Our friendship had fused, perhaps forever, on the basis of me calling him an asshole. That's what the older paper route guys called each other. Not being called an asshole meant you weren't an equal.

Harry was speechless, so he punched me in the arm, and it hurt. I winced.

"I'm sorry," he said, in earnest.

"What are you apologizing to him for," asked Estaban, suddenly appearing beside a crouching Harry. "I stopped apologizing to him when I took the top bunk six weeks ago. So how did it go?"

"He fucked up," said Harry a bit too loudly.

"Well, I know he's a fuckup, so I guess he's now an ignorant fuckup. No place like home to find commiseration. And we all know fuckups abound in this place."

"Thanks for that insightfulness. On the plus side, though, I am staying on as a, drum roll please."

No drum roll.

"Really, this is worth a drum roll."

"Okay, you got it," Thom said.

"Ta-da, a PT instructor."

"Really?" Estaban said.

"That's great," said my friend forever.

"I start Monday. Only three days away." Caught up

in the excitement of this telling, I forgot my audience. "Of course I have to get over to Sgt. Huckaby's early to pack in."

"Who's Sgt. Huckaby?" asked Estaban.

Oops. When would I learn to keep my big mouth shut? As much as I trusted them, this would not be kept a secret. It was too juicy.

"He's the sergeant I'll be staying with until my language school calls for me," I said nonchalantly.

"Here in the 96th?" asked Thom.

He gave me this look, like a dog smelling and wanting the bone I was hiding behind me. I was dead meat. Estaban could ferret out information from me in so many ways. When we played cards, he read me like a book. My "tells" proliferated under his gaze. The longer I waited to respond, the hungrier this dog would be.

"He's the sergeant Sgt. Hardin recommended I go with."

"I'd a thought you'd stay here, being Sgt. Hardin's boy and all."

"Where'd you get that idea?"

I got the "what-the-fuck-do-you-think-I am,-an-idiot?" look from Estaban.

What could he possibly know, I thought. I was

discreet. My footlocker was not full of apples for the teacher.

"What?" I said in my most convincing evasiveness.

Harry bought it, now looking at Estaban like he was on my side and unjustly interrogated. But Estaban stayed a hungry dog, staring at the bone in my hidden hand. I had to stay on this buddy-buddy rabbit trail of Sgt. Hardin and maybe he'd forget Huckaby.

"I have clipboard duty, so I've gotta see him once in awhile," I said earnestly.

"Who's this Huckabee-in-his-bonnet guy?" Estaban repeated, again with a knowing smile.

"Huckaby is just another sergeant who wants an airman third aboard to help him out with a new flight. Easy stuff, maybe march 'em to mess, I don't know." It felt like a good lie.

And better, Estaban bought it, having already made his point that he knew what was going on with Sgt. Hardin and wanted me to know he knew.

"I'm hungry. Are you guys interested in chow?" Being that we're always ready for chow, it was the perfect transition from anything else. Firmly back in the driver's seat I popped off my bunk and strutted off, my friends forever in tow.

The day we had been waiting for since our arrival

was upon us. Our last day together was spent cleaning the barracks for the incoming flight. Sgt. Hardin was in a good mood as he tacked up a duty list, in this case, his list, not mine. I got latrine duty, which was okay with me, but for the first time Bo was cleaning alongside me. His handsome features were twisted in anger.

"What are you upset for, Bo. Hell, it's only the last day of basic."

"I don't like nigger work, first day or last," he said scowling.

"I didn't make up the roster," I said defensively. "The sergeant did and maybe he saw you were getting easy duty."

"You made a deal with Jeremiah."

"There's no deal if I'm not making the roster." I knew it wouldn't placate him. There was no way to deal with his hatred of blacks. It had become a religion to him and there was no fanaticism stronger.

"I ... AIN'T ... NO ...NIGGER," he growled.

He was seething, but I didn't care. I went about cleaning the latrine, consoled with the thought that I no longer had to deal with his kind. As I scrubbed the floor on all fours, I had fleeting thoughts of Sgt. Huckaby, hovering over me with a menacing glare, when I mentally placed Bo in his latrine. What would happen to him if the sergeant heard his growling hatred. It amused me briefly, but the reality was much more foreboding. It was as if I was sitting on an open powder keg and others surrounded me flicking their cigarette lighters, their ugly smiles self-satisfied with the impending disaster. With that unsettling thought, I rose up on my knees and turned toward Bo, who was staring at me as he relaxed on one of the latrines. When our eyes met, he smiled friendly like for a second, then the smile turned hard.

"You be a nigger sweating like this."

"I don't mind hard work. You'll learn," I braved, "that the easy way out keeps you weak."

"I ain't weak. I could break your back if I wanted."

His malicious glare unnerved me. His muscles were testimony to his strength. I had seen him when doing calisthenics. He had the agility of an athlete. I had little doubt that he could overpower me. I felt that he wanted to grab me then and there regardless of the consequences. The fear he wanted to impose on me instinctively found a response, a high school ploy. "Yeah, you're strong and probably were a football quarterback and had all those cheerleaders hanging on you."

The deflection worked, his ego grabbed at my suggestion.

"I had 'em all. I mean HAD 'EM."

"I'd bet you did. Yah, all of them," I smiled as a friendly conspirator and hoped his train of thought was now off track.

But he moved stealthily toward me, like a lion to prey. I was ready to bolt, but his movement didn't unnerve me. Silently he crouched down next to me, his smile unthreatening.

In a whisper, he said, "had me two sisters, together, once." His eyebrows rose as a smile emerged. He was inches away. I waited for more on the sisters when his hand grabbed my throat, the pain shocking me and fear blooming as he struck.

"You nigger lovers are niggers, too. You got that nigger fear look now." His smile was darkly malicious, enjoying his attack.

I was tipping backward as his hold on my throat was pushing as well as pressing. My fear was overwhelming as a darkness beckoned to my helplessness. Then his hand on my throat weakened as I struck out maddeningly, flailing without recognition.

Suddenly he stopped, his hand off my throat, and a pain in my hands. The darkness lightened even as the pain persisted. Then I felt my body tugged up then lowered to a hard surface. I remained without control of my balance, sagging under my dead weight. Then arms were grasping me under my own arms. I let my body relax, fall into them. My head ached but the light increased and I heard voices.

"Can't keep out of trouble, can you?" Sgt. Hardin said peering at me from above.

I looked absently at my rescuers, who stood on each side of me, ready to catch me if I started to fall off the toilet. The pain in my head was lessening, but waves of nausea replaced it. I made a dry heave and shuddered.

"Lay him on his back, get a blanket. He's probably going into shock."

When I fully recovered my senses sitting on the toilet Estaban was standing by, his hands on my shoulders. "What a lucky bastard. You caught him both times, flush, and he cracked his head on the shitter falling."

I didn't care. All I wanted to do was lay down on my bunk. Estaban and Harry did the honors. "KO'd the sonovabitch, I swear" I heard Harry say. "Got him twice. fucker was out on his ass. It was all that boxing did it," Harry said, as I slumped to my bunk and a blanket laid over me. It was nice to have friends

The next thing I heard was Estaban's voice. "You okay?" He nudged my shoulder. When I didn't respond, he nudged again. My eyes flickered in opening.

"You'll be pleased to hear that Bodeen's getting the bum's rush out of here.

"Like what?"

"They call it unfit for military service."

"You mean after all this, he gets booted?"

"More than likely, but who gives a fuck. The turd was behind just about every bit of shit that flowed from day one. He kept pushing the white supremacy thing."

I hadn't picked up on that at all. I never quite understood what was behind it, that we never really got to working together. Even on the drill pad, we just couldn't get there. There was always something, but I had never been able to put my finger on it. The more I thought about it, words like "fuck" and "cocksucker," which were part of everyday speech, eased us into a common acceptance of each other. In the outside world they were considered the very worst of swear words. In our tension filled lives, saying at mess "to pass the fucking butter" had the humorous effect of keeping us loose. We were telling each other that we accepted each other without the fanfare of a literal meaning of acceptance. We were after all just kids, without the guile that would soon infuse our lives and separate us with a simple "wrong word." To a polite civil society fuck and cocksucker were among the worst cuss words. Now it occurred to me that the worst four letter word was hate, which casts aspersions that could cause a lifetime of bigotry between unlike sides of human endeavor. But what did I know. I was just a kid, floundering around the sea of humanity trying to keep my balance and learn something now and then.

I looked up at Leeds. "I wish he had kept his mouth shut for another day. Geez, just one day."

"His kind never give up just for a second. And don't go easy on the fucker, he hated you and let everyone know you were a pussy."

"For being different?"

"Yah, and for being a pussy. You know, Jon, your naivete sticks out like a cowlick. Any sign of weakness puts you in their sights and these guys will pull the trigger for any reason."

"You really think I'm a pussy?"

"You can't get by with lucky punches with that stiff. You're too easy going. You've got to get into control and stay there. Otherwise they'll keep taking advantage of your 'goodness' for lack of a better word.

"What's wrong with being 'good,' for the lack of a better word?"

"We're in the military if you hadn't noticed. In wartime, 'good' will get you killed every time and maybe take someone with you. In peacetime 'good' sets you up for a fall because you're not thinking how to keep from having to take the fall. Military means aggressiveness. Take no prisoners. Either you are a weathered soldier or a victim and/or casualty. There are few exceptions. You may be one of them. But take heed, my friend, many of these guys eat their own."

Chapter Twelve

I was nervous as I approached Sgt. Huckaby's barracks, all my belongings in the blue duffel bag that hung from my shoulder as I trudged my way to it. I felt like a raw recruit despite the single stripe attached to my blouse that proclaimed me a survivor of basic training. A youngster was on duty at the front door as I approached it. When we made eye contact, I felt very much as young and typically naïve as he looked. It was probably his first duty as a door guard, having a bewildered look on his hairless baby face. That notion calmed me and gave me the edge that Sgt. Hardin had tried to instill in me earlier. "Just remember not to judge others or underestimate them by what you see," he said in his taciturn manner as I slung my duffel bag onto my shoulder.

"Airman Third Class Breckenridge to see the sergeant," I bellowed with authority.

"Who? I mean, ah, what," stammered the nervous recruit.

I unslung the duffel bag as I mounted the stairs and

stood before him, separated by the screened door. "Tell the sergeant that Airman Third Class Breckenridge is here."

"Whall," he said, "he's not here," which seemed to satisfy him that he was no longer responsible for what he didn't know.

"In that case, just let me in and when the sergeant returns, you can tell him I am inside."

"I can do that?"

"Yep, that's the procedure," I assured him.

He reached to unhook the clasp when a voice behind him turned him away.

For a nervous second I considered that Sgt. Huckaby had returned and was about to loom before me, a scowl on his massive black face, but it turned out to be another recruit who carried a bit of authority in his voice.

"The sergeant told us to 'hold tight' until he returns," said the dark-haired recruit who faced me.

It was very close to 1700 hours and I was reminded not to be late, but now his guy wasn't cooperating. "The sergeant is expecting me," I said calmly, though I was beginning to tense up. As I slowly breathed while the recruit made up his mind, he decided a dilemma had arisen. "He didn't say anything about anyone coming in," he said flatly.

"He may have forgotten, but I was told to be here no later than 1700 hours, and that was what he ordered, so let me in." As soon as that last phrase was uttered, I knew I was done for. It was wimpy and welcomed the challenge he was about to give to it."

He rephrased his position to "hold tight," which meant I wasn't about to get in unless I controlled our discourse.

"I'm sure Sgt. Huckaby meant that after I arrived, which is what I was ordered to do by 1700, everything should be locked down for the evening, you understand."

"Just who are you?"

"Open the fucking door," I yelled.

"I can't do that," he said, stiffening.

"Listen to this then. I am assigned to this flight for the next six weeks to assist the sergeant in his training of YOU. I will be living here and you will be taking orders from me as you would Sgt. Huckaby. Is that any clearer?"

"Just a second," dark hair said, and then closed the door.

I was fuming as the seconds ticked by. I even

considered that Sgt. Huckaby was inside, testing them to follow his orders to the letter, and thereby testing me. It was beginning to make sense. It was a challenge to see how I responded. I had my doubts that these untrained recruits would risk angering anyone in their first day of training. With that thought I was sure the sergeant was inside. A fire drill was standard operating procedure the first night, so he had to be in. All this conjecture didn't calm me, however. It seemed Machiavellian. I was on the verge of humiliation just to make a point. I stared at the closed door before me until a noise broke into my reverie. I turned. A staff sergeant from the barracks across was standing on his porch with arms akimbo and grimacing at me.

"Is there a problem?" he barked.

I wasn't sure what to say in the way of an explanation, but at least it was someone who could recommend what to do, so I walked to the pathway between us, holding eye contact all the way.

"I was ordered by Sgt. Huckaby to be here no later than 1700 hours. I am his new assistant until my training school can take me. But they won't let me in the barracks. I'm told he said to 'hold tight' until he returned, but they misunderstood what he meant by it."

I was satisfied with my explanation and felt back in control.

"Well, airman, what don't you understand about

holding tight. I tell my boys to 'hold tight,' they better hold tight and not let anyone in."

"But I was told by Sgt. Hardin that Sgt. Huckaby wanted me here no later than five o'clock."

"There's no five o'clock in the military, boy. It's 1700 hours, or didn't your TI train you right."

I had gotten myself into a nasty situation which seemed to worsen as I tried to wiggle free.

"Yes, sergeant, I know that. It's just that ..."

"I don't need to hear any more of your misunderstanding. Get on back to where you came from. Hold tight means hold tight." With that he shook his head, turned and pulled on his front door, which did not open. "Open the damn door," he yelled. He turned back at me, glared and blurted, "git on," and shook his head as the door opened and he burst in, barking at the door guard on the way.

I trudged back to Sgt. Hardin's barracks. After two months of cold winds and chilly days, March weather was comfortable and even hot on some days. The temperature was in the 80s and humid. I was perspiring. I looked forward to my first day of calisthenics the following day in warm weather. I knew the routine and was confident that nothing would go wrong. I had convinced myself that I was back on square one, blocking out anything that would disrupt a smooth eight weeks with Sgt. Huckaby.

My naiveté was overwhelming.

Sgt. Hardin heard me come in and yelled, "Back so soon."

I felt like the ball in a pinball game, being knocked around for the amusement of some military gods. But worse, I felt the naiveté that everyone doused me with. I felt utterly weak, but managed to respond.

"How do you know … or, what do you know … that I don't." I voiced my complaint to a barren barracks, in which a lower god occupied unseen.

"I can tell from your voice that you are taking this badly. To answer, I know everything, as you surely must know by now," Sgt. Hardin's voice said, followed by his appearance, "but this bit of information came to me just after you left, and I didn't feel like running after you, you understand."

I was on the verge of spilling tears, an accumulation of anxiety and disappointment. I understood, but didn't. I wanted him to do something to convey that he cared enough for me to have made the effort to get me that information. I felt warm and my rising emotions were on display, targeting me for his typical retort to 'buckle up.' I searched for some understanding in his brown eyes and wry smile.

"Ease up, Timmy."

"Damn it, I'm no Timmy," I blurted as tears flowed. I couldn't prevent my loss of control. I felt picked on and abandoned.

Sgt. Hardin approached consolingly, and placed a hand on my back, like my mom did.

"Grip up," his soothing voice said.

I felt the warmth of his hand on my back and felt a flush of relief. My tears slowed to a stop as my eyes tried to focus.

"Sgt. Williams had just come from HQ and passed on a message from Sgt. Huckaby saying he would be detained and had put a 'hold tight' on. What you have to do is stop by the squadron HQ to get a pass through the hold tight. See the desk sergeant. Jon, you have to relax and not take things you can't control personally."

There it was. It caught my ear and set off a deep-seated need I sought from my supposedly loving parents or anyone I cared about: A reciprocal caring, in the absence of love shown. He showed he cared about me simply by using my first name, which is strictly forbidden between TIs and their charges. I was overwhelmed and the spreading warmth I felt comforted me greatly.

He sensed something which he conveyed by a cocking of his head. "Are you alright?"

"Yeah," I sighed.

"Then what you should do is see Sgt. Huckaby tomorrow when you are finished with your physical training exercises. Take my word on this, Jon. You have to stay in control of your ..., of yourself. Show any sign of weakness and you'll be treated as weak. You never, and I mean never, let them think they can make you flinch. As for Huckaby, he will eat you alive."

He paused and I waited and thought about what leaving my home of the past eight weeks would be like. I would be on my own again. No more trips back here. If we meet, our exchanges would be cordial and short.

"That first encounter when you stood up for Leeds. I should have booted you. Actually I had to, given the circumstances. If it ever got around that I let a recruit get away with that I'd be ruined. My fraternal brotherhood would never let me forget it. Some would hate me and show it."

I couldn't let him go on. Suddenly I felt ashamed for what I had done that first day. I had jeopardized his career for my sense of justice, a fair play gesture that somehow always ended up as a blunder. It was a weakness that I should risk everything for someone I didn't even know. I was ready to apologize, but didn't get my chance.

"Your willingness to take the fall reminded me of a youngster I once knew or thought I knew until he had to make a hard choice that could change his life forever. He made it and survived the hurt feelings that came from it."

It may have been him or someone close to him that he was talking about. But it didn't matter. It was important that he understood the meaning of making hard choices as a young man. It showed by the quaver in his voice, an emotional pulse that trips when a certain depth is reached. I understood, finally. I braced to attention, relieving him of further conversation.

"Thank you, Sgt. Hardin, for … your assistance in all my endeavors.

"Endeavors, my butt. Get the FU outa here."

I leaned over to grasp my duffel bag, but Sgt. Hardin beat me to it. He hefted it to my shoulder, and patted my back. We walked silently to the front door, which he opened and stepped aside as I departed. I wobbled on the steps and nearly fell, but regained my own balance and stepped to the pavement. I needn't have looked to see Sgt. Hardin shaking his head in bewilderment.

I felt ready to take another adventure, perhaps one I would never forget for the right reasons. As I left my barracks it was cool at 0630 hours, a slight breeze out of the south hinting at a warmer day ahead. With my duffle bag slung over my shoulder I began my second trip to Sgt. Huckaby's barracks.

I got the pass quite easily. No long exchanges. Brevity was becoming my style. As I approached my new home, and a new address 8034, my confidence was brimming. A new door guard was standing away from the door talking to another recruit when I stepped up to the wooden door and knocked. He turned quickly, a worried look on his face, and hurried to the door. He was less than brief, he had nothing to say as he stood on the other side of the door.

I hesitated, peering directly at him, waiting for a response.

Dead silence and no apparent curiosity brought me to bring the pass into view.

I expected a "hold tight" reply or some acknowledgment, but he continued to gawk at me.

"Open the door," I said nonchalantly.

Effortlessly he reached out and unhooked the door and pushed it toward me. I was at a loss of just what to do then. He was dead meat. At that moment the boy's life was in my hands. Thoughts may have passed, but their speed was too quick to comprehend. I deftly pushed the door closed, with little resistance from the door guard.

"When someone comes to the door, you are to ask who they are and what they want. My answer would be that I am expected by your TI and have a pass that releases his 'hold tight' command. At that time you should ask me to bring the pass closer so you can read it. If at anytime you are doubtful of what to do next, you can ask someone else on your side of the door."

I pressed the pass to the screen door.

He leaned forward and peered at it, but stayed noncommittal. I waited

"You can come in now, I think."

"I will," I said and opened the door as he stepped back. Once inside, I suggested he let Sgt. Huckaby know he had a visitor. Again he was stumped. "Say the words," I prompted.

"A visitor for Sgt. Huxabee," he yelled.

"Huckaby, not Huxabee," I whispered.

"Who is it?" The big voice fit the man.

"Tell him, Airman Breckenridge."

"Airman Beckinbridge."

"Let him in," Huckaby blared.

"He is."

"He is what?"

"He's already in, sir."

I heard him before he appeared at the top of the steps. It sounded like uncoordinated stomps, as if he had just woken up and hadn't stretched. Suddenly a sheet of white appeared, which turned out to be his underwear. His blackness was subdued by the poor lighting atop the stairs; his eyes seeming to bulge out of the blackness. The eyes glared at me with malicious intent, then quickly softened as did his countenance.

"Did you do the crossword puzzle?"

He saw confusion spread across my face.

"Sunday's Times puzzle?"

"Ah, no. I've been too busy. I don't really --- get the time," I said lamely as he turned back into his room.

I had been dismissed before welcomed but I didn't let it get to me. I hefted the duffle bag on my shoulder and stepped toward the bay, where dozens of recruits stared at me. I made eye contact with some and found among them those who were proprietary about their personal space, which I had just entered. From the look "invaded" was the proper verb. I guess I hesitated too long to respond, because I saw a smirk from one, his eyes piercing and certainly not warm, nor friendly.

I stared back into a stiff connection with those dark penetrating eyes, and weakly held onto them for a few seconds, thoughtful of Sgt. Hardin's admonition "not to flinch."

"I'll see you for calisthenics. I'll get you in shape or else," I blurted loudly, but without conviction." I turned away and disappeared into the assistant's room, hoping that I had regained some measure of pride.

I was in the middle of getting settled in when someone knocked on my door. I opened it to find a tall, gangling blond boy, with a protruding Adam's apple, standing there.

"I was to tell you that Sgt. Huckaby wants to see you."

His accent sounded Appalachian, quite similar to Braxton and Loy, my former flight mates. He had that country boy look.

"What's your name?" I asked.

"What?"

"Your name. What is it?"

"My whole name?"

"Sure, why not."

"Francis Dornwall. Well it's really Dorwalski, but my pappy changed it when he come here from Poland. We's Polish."

"Your pappy work in the mines?"

"How'd you know that. You from Poland?"

"Nope, but I have friends who are from West Virginia. Their fathers worked the mines.

"In Poland?"

"Oh, so your father worked in the mines in Poland?"

"That was a long time ago. He got hurt. Then we came to America. My father works in No. 2."

"I guess that's a coal mining company, but didn't you say he got hurt?"

"My pappy, not my father."

"Here, in America, a pappy is a father, not a grandfather," I explained . "From what you've told me, your grandfather got hurt working in the mines in Poland and your father works in the mines here in America, in No. 2."

Francis nodded, which I took to be an affirmation of my understanding.

Out of that rambling conversation, Francis seemed to be a happy-go-lucky can-do type who took things as they were and survived adversity. Yet I felt a simplicity about him that fit the Abbott and Costello routine we had just concluded. There was no guile in him, but a weakness more than intellect. His overt friendliness made him the perfect foil for the soon to be determined leadership, who were probably feeling out who belonged "in" their social register. He would need some support and guidance from the other "outs," who were potential victims. I was prepared to help on that score, when he apparently read my mind.

"Can I be your friend? I don't have any friends here yet."

"Sure. And as a friend, can I call you Frank?"

"I guess so, if you want."

"Is Frank, I mean, does anyone call you Frank?"

"No. Name's Francis."

I decided on some privacy, and asked Francis to come into my room, but kept the door open. He looked around and then walked over to my cot. He dug in his pants pocket and came up with a quarter. I knew what he was up to, and hoped the blanket had some spring in it. He flipped the coin over the bunk. It hit the blanket and bounced. Francis smiled.

"That's real important. Sgt. Huckaby told me so. He wants to know everything I do." He tole me we were friends."

"Just how did that come about?" I inquired, already sure what was forthcoming.

"What?"

"I'm sorry. How did you and Sgt. Huckaby become

friends so early after getting here?"

"I got pushed into it, sorta." Frank was self-satisfied with his answer as I was clueless, so I asked for more information. He explained that Sgt. Huckaby got upset with the flight at their first encounter. Someone said something while he was explaining his status as God. He inquired who was talking. Then someone pushed him in the back and he stumbled forward. Frank's cloak of anonymity was pulled that instant. I knew the rest having been there in my first encounter with Sgt. Hardin. That friendship became real through a diligence that won him over. One could only hope that Frank would survive his "friendship" with Sgt. Huckaby.

"Now let's get back to your name, Frank. "In America, we often have nicknames, like my birth name is Jonathon, but I answer to Jon. We shorten the names to something easier to say. Frank sounds better than your name Francis, which sounds like a girl's name, Frances, which is spelled differently but sounds the same. Frank is a man's name, Francis sounds like a girl's name and people in the military like men's names for men.

"Garrett calls me Dork."

"Who is Garrett?"

"He's a squad leader. Sgt. Huckaby made him one."

I would have to keep an eye out for this Garrett, who might be another Bo.

"I'm going to call you Frank. You said it was alright. I want you to call yourself Frank, not Francis. Okay?" I'll ask Sgt. Huckaby to call you Frank, too. Is that okay with you?"

"Okey-dokey. That's what my daddy say to Ma when everything is going well.

"I'm going up to see Sgt. Huckaby. Whenever someone calls you anything other than Frank, you tell them your name is Frank." I ushered Frank out of my room and eyed the bay for inquisitive eyes. No one was paying attention. I followed Frank upstairs and stopped before Sgt. Huckaby's door. I rapped lightly.

"Come in."

My conversation with Frank put me in a confident mood, and confidence is what I needed for my upcoming encounter. I opened the door to find Sgt. Huckaby sprawled at his desk in his underwear with a paper in one hand and a pencil poised in the air with the other.

"Take this laundry," he began, pointing his pencil toward a duffle bag of what I guessed to be laundry, "and go heavy on the bleach. I want my clothes smelling clean." With that, he turned his attention back to his crossword puzzle and tapped his teeth with the pencil.

I had been dismissed, but refused to budge. I held my ground silently and watched him like prey to a voracious predator. There in the grip of his will a thought came to me. This was truly a mind game, he at his crossword yet thinking of how to get to me, to keep me off balance. I was sure I was right when he moved imperceptibly, preparing to fire another volley at me. I jumped on it and our words clashed.

"I have a PT class and will ...," I began assertively.

"Are you still here?" he said, jerking around to face me.

"I was about to explain that ..."

"Git on with it and remember to go heavy on the bleach."

"I'll be back at 1500. I'll put them there," indicating with my eyes where the duffel laid."

"No," he said authoritatively. "You stay out of my room. Leave it outside the door."

Okey dokey was on my lips, a familiarity I knew would get to him, when I bit my tongue. This was the worst time to get familiar. I had to pick my moments. This was not one of them. "Yes sergeant," I said subserviently. Without another word, I grabbed the bag and slung it over my back and left.

Chapter Thirteen

The base's parade grounds were situated adjacent to the drill pads used by our squadron. While each squadron had its own drill pads, or shared them with another, they were separate from the parade grounds, unless adjacent to it. This large open field was mindful of a high school's oval track, inside of which was a football field. The difference was size. The parade field was four times the size, or a mile oval. It could handle at least four PT classes at the same time without physical or aural interference to each other. The 98th Squadron's PT classes were held in the southeast corner. In each sector there stood movable six-foot high platforms, on which the PT instructors stood to conduct their classes.

I was standing on mine, while four flights wearing dark pink shorts and white t-shirts, were heading my way. Another class, held in the northwest corner, was underway, the sounds of which were faint. I watched as the flights moved slowly toward me, like an army marching to battle. I felt a little anxiety as they neared. If done right, they could come in as one large phalanx and stop roughly 10 yards from me in a straight line.

Occasionally the PT instructor could take over the drill call and march them in. This was not the case this time.

I immediately recognized Sgt. Huckaby's voice as he seamlessly mobilized his fledgling flight in between two other approaching flights. The fourth flight's TI looked familiar, then surprised me, as Sgt. Hardin's lean frame loomed into closer view as it made an end around to fill in the phalanx on one side. When the barking orders were completed, four flights were standing before me. Roughly 240 recruits had their eyes on me. The sergeants silently moved toward the platform, as I prepared to move them apart with drilling instructions. As they loomed before me I caught Sgt. Hardin looking up at me as he approached from my left side. My anxiety surged as all eyes waited on me. What I was waiting for I wasn't sure, but my voice hadn't come to me. I stood there waiting for some kind of inspiration. It came somewhere below me, from a known source.

"Git on it, boy. Got a tight schedule," boomed Sgt. Huckaby.

It sounded like a squawk as I blurted out my command to them to move an arm's length apart. Then I commanded all but the first row to take two steps backward.

They executed, but not without some commentary.

"Silence in the ranks," I barked, quickly trying to assert my control.

"Well, at least they's still on the field," said Sgt. Huckaby, followed by some chuckling from the two other sergeants. "What's you doing here, Hardon?"

"Brackett's back in the dentist's chair."

"Boyz got no backbone, else he be here wid the boys."

They continued their chatter, but I was not listening. I yelled for side straddle hops on my count. "One."

They sprung into action, somewhat haphazardly as a few hadn't moved at all.

"Halt," I bellowed, and heard some snickering below, which I ignored.

"Everyone together, and pay attention or else you'll be giving me two laps on the track."

"Uuuw," came a duet chorus below me, then a snappy reply from Sgt. Hardin.

"You knuckleheads plan on giving the boy a chance?" It was not a question and didn't invite a retort. None came.

I recalled for side straddle hops and got a uniform response. Everyone was on the same page. For the next half hour, I drilled them with calisthenics. I noticed those lagging to my left failed miserably on my four count pushups, having difficulty getting their overweight bodies in cadence. They would soon be fodder for the track. I was prepared to have them run to get in shape. I was feeling more in control, my confidence swelling when I put them at ease and asked the sergeants if they were staying for open field games.

Sgt. Hardin and another said no. They left to go to their flights. Once they had them move out, I dismissed the two remaining flights, telling them where to reassemble.

"I'm going to run some in your flight, Sgt. Decker. Any objections?

"Run 'em," he said.

I reiterated the same intention to Sgt. Huckaby.

"You sure you wanna do that?"

"Not unless you want to do it, yourself, sergeant."

"Touche," said Sgt. Huckaby.

His word use caught my attention. Rarely was I surprised when any sergeant said anything. It was usually terse and pointed. Anything other than uniform remarks alerted me to an individuality beyond the norm, and I was unprepared for incongruities. Before I could respond, Huckaby told me to "go ahead."

I eased off the platform and approached those in Sgt. Decker's flight I had chosen to run a lap. I pointed at them individually and told them to run a lap. "If I see you walking, you'll take another lap."

Disgruntled, they broke ranks and started jogging.

I eyeballed the squad leaders in Sgt. Huckaby's flight. I got some defiant looks, but decided not to add them to those I had already chosen. A few when pointed at, did not move. I told them to move, but they stood their ground.

"Do as the boy says," said the sergeant, as if weary of the matter.

I was on dangerous ground now, stung with dismissal of my grade and control of my order. I felt provoked and anger rose in me like a flue. I turned toward Sgt. Huckaby.

"Sergeant, respectfully, I am not your 'boy.' I am an Airman Third Class instructor trying to do his job."

His black hole eyes stared at me, but I had no sense of what I had stirred up within him, but didn't particularly care. His granite countenance held no tells. I felt disconnected from the reality around me, unafraid of the fear I should possess for the situation.

"What kind of games you plan on having for my boys, Airman Third Class Breckinridge?"

"I haven't decided."

"I have a suggestion." He smiled with the confidence of knowing the game better than the opposition.

I knew I was overmatched, so I waited out on that precipice I had inched out on many times before. I felt the dryness of my throat squeeze my mind and numbness shrink my resolve. I tilted my head like a dog.

"Box-ing. Toe to toe."

A surge of relief wetted my tongue.

"I can take a punch for the sake of character building, I suspect."

"With gloves on, you have to be, or else you'll be punished for your mistakes. You do make mistakes, Airman Third Class Breckinridge?"

"Every day, sergeant, and hoping for some guidance along the way."

"Enough chatter. That's what it is, isn't it? Nothing of substance."

"Quite the opposite. I am trying to figure out who and what I am."

He smiled, and suddenly the massive black hole lightened up, a hint of color filtered in. "Do as Airman Third Class Breckinridge ordered. Now git."

I turned and moved toward his flight, scanning the

faces of those I had chosen before. One tall squad leader, Hughie Wallace, a Detroiter, smiled widely. I looked past him to those I had picked out earlier. On their own, they moved out, and ran when I yelled for them to run.

"Follow me," I ordered the others, with a wave of my hand, and started for the equipment storage case.

My thoughts turned to the mottled grass before me. It was now largely rich green. A month ago it was a dormant light brown. I thought of the cycles of botanical life, then considered how its mottled color characterized the inherent differences in us as we cycled through life. I was among a phalanx of struggling youth of a variety of backgrounds that were ordered on a daily basis to change their identities, to conform to a new set of rules not of their making in order to think alike in a crisis, should it come to that. My thoughts focused on what we did daily as a unit, how we responded to orders. It was a steady drill meant to follow a pattern of response in preparation of fulfilling an order. A drill was, simply, an order. It was a mindset that transcended our societal differences and focused on a particular goal.

Separating the man from the drill, I realized how different these TIs were, and in particular how Sgt. Huckaby maintained control over his recruits. I thought at first sight it was fear of him. Now I wasn't sure. There was a lot more to him than I would have thought.

My thoughts were interrupted as a football bounced in front of me. Awakened from my reverie, I deftly picked it up and looked up.

"Come on, throw it," yelled someone my size. Others participating looked at me, in judgment of my capabilities.

I waved my arm, indicating I wanted someone to run in that direction. A black man began a sprint about 40 yards away. Aiming my throw, the ball spun out of my grip and flew 10 yards ahead of him in a medium arc. In a last second burst of speed he snatched it, and whooped gloriously. In turn he swept his arm and others ran to catch his pass. He threw a bullet pass of 20 yards, but the receiver failed to hold onto it.

"Do we have to play football?" asked a short stubby recruit.

"Nope. There's a bat and ball in there," I said, pointing to the storage bin. "There should be a volleyball and net, too."

He swaggered over to the bin, which was open, and peered in as if expecting to find a rattlesnake awaiting an innocent arm. Then slowly he bent over and reached in, extracting a bat and ball. Stepping back, he declared his intention to hit to someone and sought volunteers. "Anyone for 500," he yelled. A couple dozen recruits were grouped together just standing around. No one took him up. I saw his disappointment.

"I'll play," I said, and moved off in the opposite direction as the football players, who now had doubled in participants. Hopefully soon, they would play a game of touch.

I ran out deep enough to catch 150 foot flies. I turned just in time for him to make a ferocious swing and miss. And miss. And miss. On his fourth swing he hit a dribbler out 40 feet. He didn't move to retrieve it, nor did I.

"You're closer. Get it," I yelled.

Reluctantly he lumbered for it. Rather than return to his original spot, he swung from there, and connected. I watched the long fly arc past me, and looked discouragingly at him. "Asshole," I muttered, and ran after the ball. I threw the ball into him on one hop. He missed the catch. The ball ran into the non-players, bouncing off a leg or two. A tall recruit picked it up and looked in my direction. I pointed to the batter. Instead of throwing it to him, he ran over to the batter and reached out for the bat. The short recruit said no.

"Give me the fucking bat." It drew the attention of the non-players who were dispersing in all direction. Some ran out toward me, while the argument who was batter continued. The tall squad leader won and waved me back. I backpedaled to 250 feet and watched the newcomers find a spot to wait for a hit ball. The squad leader, who had the look of an athlete, took a couple practice swings. I began to drift further back.

His first swing connected and soared overhead to my right. I sped off and made an easy catch on the run. I made the long throw into him on a single bounce.

"Nice arm," he yelled. Another long fly was directly overhead and was easily catchable.

I yelled out: "200."

He nodded and hit a pop up purposefully to get another player 100 points.

After scattering a few grounders and a sneak long ball, which I caught, he must have figured it was better for me to bat than the others. He hit two consecutive long balls to me and then a towering fly. The player in front of me was wavering as the ball plummeted. He misjudged it, but I hadn't. A catch put me at 500 and the next batter.

As I finished my run in, the squad leader started running out, nodding as he passed me. When I turned, I saw a dozen players in the outfield, among them Frank. I thought this would be interesting. I began scattering them with long fly balls, all in the 250 feet range. On each catch a whoop went up. Frank was playing very deep. I decided to see if he could show me something positive. With a slight swing alteration, my next fly was high and long and right at him. He brought his hands up, but I could see his movements were uneven, as if he was rolling on the deck of a floundering ship. The ball went over his head in his futile reach, and he followed the grab with a flop on his butt. More whoops replied, but now discouragingly.

I yelled out, asking for scores. One fleet runner yelled back 400. I smacked one high and long and watched his sprint toward it. Two others ran from different angles. I was rooting for the speedster, but he missed as a tall recruit grabbed it. I motioned Frank to come in much closer

I hit a long fly in the opposite direction to them. The speedster quickly ran toward it, but was called off by one closer as the ball began its descent. The ball was caught by the caller. I could hear the infectious rivalry among the deeper players. They all acknowledged good catches and didn't interfere on any calls. The speedster was determined to win and ran for every ball I hit. My last ball was a line drive center to all outfielders. Frank stumbled forward. I suddenly feared the ball might nail him as he awkwardly converged on it. Out of nowhere the speedster swooped in front of him and snagged the ball. Frank tried to stop his momentum but failed and fell amid whoops for the speedster and, seconds later, jeers for the fall.

"Nice wheels," I blurted to the speedster as he raced by as I ran out to the fallen albatross. No one else seemed to care that Frank had splattered head first to hard ground.

He was on his feet by the time I reached him.

"I'm not too good at this, but it's a great game, ain't it," he burbled.

"You bleeding Frank?"

"Don't matter, I'm not much good running. My pop says I got heavy feet."

"Do me a favor.

"What's that?"

Don't try boxing."

"My brothers and me always wrestling and such. They try not to hurt me." He grinned goofishly, a distorted smile made up of odd angles and crooked teeth, but a warm smile nevertheless. There was something endearing about him. A big innocent target for ridicule, and harassment. "Be careful, will ya?" I said, moving off. I trotted back to the hitter, who waited for me before hitting.

"He's okay, but took a nasty spill," I said.

"Does that regular, it seems. You see him in the shower?"

"Huh?"

"He looks like he gets the blanket, not like he deserves it, but ... ".

"You sure?" A deep anger flared.

"Word like that gets around. I'm on the first, so I never seen or heard anything. Been told you can hear a moaner, but like I said, we're on different floors.

"Who's doing it?" My anger coated the question.

"Don't know."

"Gimme a guess." I was sure but I didn't want to jump to my gut feeling. Frank's beating hovered uneasily on the first floor of my subconscious.

"Some guys have a problem with higher ups. You're on a shit list or two."

"Already? Usually it takes a couple of days before I get under someone's skin."

"After seeing you swing that bat, I doubt they'll fuck with you. Those kind need easy targets."

"I know." I mulled that over. If I went to bat for Dornwall I'd have to be on high alert while watching my own back. Well, thanks for the heads up" You gotta name?"

"Miller."

"Again, I appreciate that, Miller. I noticed he was focused on the outfielders. "Make every swing count, and run 'em ragged." I headed off for the inactive group, whose numbers were about a dozen.

"Got nothing to do?" I blurted as I walked among them. "Got boxing gloves in the bin." I didn't intend for it to be a personal invitation, but I could see it may have been taken that way. I knew that look, had seen it on that first meeting with Sgt. Huckaby.

"What's your name?" I asked Dark Eyes, who carried a cockiness like a badge of honor. He was about 6-2 and maybe 180, with reddish blond hair. I would have said he was handsome, with a lantern jaw and high check bones, if not for his eyes. They were broodingly dark blue-grey, that reminded me of a wolf.

"Garrett."

No surprise there. Garrett had the menacing look of a predator, sorting out the species into categories: strong and weak. In the weak grouping was Frank, who I knew was out throwing the football. I looked for Frank. I spied him making an ungainly lope for a pass that was dropped, a kick of disgust and then an amiable show of hands that his hands, not him, were to blame. At least there he was safe.

"We've got horseshoes, badminton, volleyball. You don't like those, you can run the track." I said this without eye contact, like a teacher explaining the curriculum.

We got to the bin.

"Your choice," I said flatly.

"I'll take the gloves," Garrett said.

"Get 'em. Someone got a watch? They're one minute rounds, no more than two or three rounds." I saw Garrett smile wolfishly as he hefted the heavily padded gloves. I turned away, in dismissal of any further involvement.

"Hey," called out Garrett.

I ignored him.

"Hey, you," he barked.

He was getting to me with his superior attitude, but I choked it down and walked on.

I didn't hear him approach until he was alongside me.

"Hey, I'm talking to you," he said, grabbing my arm not gently.

I turned to face him while trying to wrench my left arm free. His grip was very strong. I looked up and felt a surging fear that engulfed me as dark malevolent eyes claimed me. There was nowhere to go. He seemed to be squeezing me into submission, like a dominant wolf with clenched teeth on the neck of another, ready to tear at the slightest resistance. I could not bear to feel this overwhelming advantage, which gave rise to nausea and deepening weakness. I could feel the tears begin to well and my pride spill away. I knew this was a death grip by an instinct carried through generations of flesh and bone: kill or be killed. Without further thought, I struck out, wailing my fist until I struck flesh and bone. I was released, but couldn't stop thrashing out blindly, my heart pumping erratically. My fist made contact again and Garrett suddenly loomed before me. Garrett's face stared at me incredulously as my pumping right arm brought a vicious fist to his face, and then a left that missed. I was swinging wildly until I was grabbed from behind and twisted away. My fear faded as the constraint held me without pain.

"Slow down, boy, you got a tiger by the tail," soothed Sgt. Huckaby. "Juss ease up there, git ahold of yourself." His voice was soft and reassuring.

I felt my control easing back in, my heartbeat abating. His large hands were now comforting as they steadied me. As his grip loosened, I felt less secure, wanting his control.

"Tha's better."

Then I was on my own, his hands freeing me. I wobbled a little as my full consciousness returned.

"You okay?" His voice was now harder and I knew he wasn't talking to me.

Garrett was standing just beyond arm's length, his face red.

"The punk couldn't hurt me if he tried," he blurted, then tried to laugh it off, but the affect didn't come off. He looked unsteady and the redness on his cheekbone was flaming. He tried to regroup himself when another recruit came to his aid, gripping his arm to steady him.

He jerked away. "Leggo." He stared at me, his face a mask of malevolence.

I saw his hatred and realized we had become natural enemies. I had to watch my step now. I couldn't rely on Sgt. Huckaby rescuing me the next time, and I was sure Garrett would be looking for an opportunity to get back at me.

We dispersed, going our separate ways. I saw Miller looking at me and making a facial gesture that he'd told me what to expect. Then he smiled, and I felt maybe I had some friends to back me up if and when Garrett and his group came at me.

Chapter Fourteen

It was apparent to me that the routine of basic training kept my enemies at arm's length. I encountered no forays to get me in the following week. Those, like Miller, who were friendly, seemed to have an effect on my opposition, keeping them at bay. They were a loose protectorate of sorts, watching my back, while easing into the rigors of Sgt. Huckaby's personality.

I hadn't yet figured out the big man but I was getting closer. It was a cleaning day, which meant grousing started early. Sgt. Huckaby had a brief meeting with his squad leaders to explain what he expected: nothing less than cleanliness that would pass a white glove inspection.

The squad leaders were geographically mixed: Harley Thompkins from Texas, Detroiter Hughie Wallace, Californian Gerald Massey and New Yorker Sam Johnston, and had only one thing in common. They were chosen because of their tall height, which fit a look Sgt. Huckaby wanted when drilling or marching: short in front, tall in back.

They came out of Huckaby's room with mixed responses, mostly anxious perplexity.

I held my hand out to stop them. "Don't get down guys," I suggested. There's an easy solution." I was amused by the consternation I saw.

"Yah, sure," lamented 2nd squad leader Wallace, who looked constantly beleaguered.

"Easy as pie," I piped knowingly.

"Don't say soap and hot water, cause that what he say."

I nodded with a smile.

"It's simple and easy. First, get some buckets and washing gloves from HQ while setting up the barracks. Clear out one side of everything and scrub it clean, then do the other side. One squad moving, the other cleaning. Get done in maybe two hours. Then make sure no one comes in the bay with dirty shoes. Have 'em take their shoes off outside and clean them before entering."

I dunno," said Francis, who was standing behind me.

"What don't you know?" I was about to say Francis, but caught myself and inserted Frank instead, but it came out wrong, a little too harsh and the impact on him was immediate. He shrank in front of my eyes, withdrawing into a well worn shell where no harm would come him.

I tried to apologize, but he remained stunned by my verbal misstep. The transformation worried me, but also annoyed me. How anyone could be so sensitive made me wonder how he had survived so far. Instinctively, I placed a hand on his crossed arms in a maternal show of caring, while turning my attention to the others.

"NO," he blurted in an anguished cry, pushing my hand away.

"Hey, Frank, ease up." It came from Hughie Wallace. He gave Frank a backhand swipe to his shoulder. "He didn't mean anything by it," he said, then adding as he turned to me, "didja?"

I nodded no.

"I didn't hear you." Hughie's meaning was unequivocal.

"No, Frank. It's just that you take everything so personal that ..."

"Tha's okay. Frank's havin' a tough day an it goin' to be tougher he don't shape up." Hughie smiled as he eyed Frank, who instantly melted on command, settling back to his homey disposition. In seconds he was grinning.

"We get it shipshape," Hughie said, swinging his arm the breadth of the bay. "You," he pointed to Frank, get the water and make sure it's hot. Don't spill it."

Frank loped off with a grin.

"I know you wasn't mad at him, but you right. Frank's a worry cause he don't think. He always ready to step back, let everyone step up on him."

"Francis is really a nice guy." I began, but hesitated when Hughie eyed me sternly, telling me an explanation wasn't necessary. So I let it go.

I stood by nonchalantly while the work crews went about mopping and cleaning the barracks. I roamed each floor to oversee their efforts, but stayed clear of Garrett and his crew, who were avoiding any serious work while quick to comment on how poorly those working were doing.

In passing by Sgt. Huckaby's open door, which was a rarity, I glimpsed him sitting at a desk facing the door, but peering at something quizzically. I stopped, seeing what that something was. A crossword puzzle. I hesitated, trying to figure out if I dared an encounter. He raised his head up and stared somewhat in my direction as he tried to find the word he was looking for while gazing about in deep thought. I began to pull away when his eyes suddenly locked on mine. I stood there muted until a slow smile rose and his countenance changed to accept my presence.

"I 'member you say you do the puzzle."

I nodded, and he instantly nodded for me to enter.

I was drawn to his side, eager to see how he was doing. His inserts were few and far between. It was not encouraging and I didn't like thinking he was out of his element, or maybe even worse, on the stupid side.

He pointed to 12 Down with a stubby pencil. The clue was "unexplained sighting" for a three letter word. I had a guess, but double-checked it with the adjoining across word to see a match of the same letter. It fit. Rather than just say it, I gave him a hint, letting him figure it out. "It's not of this world," I said.

Whatever was going on in his head hadn't figured it out. He had a pained expression on his face. He grimaced, which caused me to think of another clue. As I was ready to spill it out, Sgt. Huckaby quietly smiled and penciled in the letters U, F, O. His smile widened into an expanse of white teeth.

I learn who the real Huckaby is with the help of Sgt. Hardin, who I helps me understand that Cletus does his job his way. "Can you scare people into doing what you want them to do?" I ask. "No, but it is a sure way of getting their attention. Don't underestimate what he is capable of doing. He gets very good results.

Meeting Sgt. Huckaby: the ground rules, duties, expectations that slip out day by day so casually.

After bringing him his bleached (heavily) whites, I notice a checkerboard, but no checkers. Subsequently I inquire and ask to play a game. Eventually he says it's for chess, not checkers. He gets around to saying that he's trying to play chess better. I say I play some, too, and if he'd like a game, I'd oblige.

Another time, he says.

Then I buy him a chess book and try to explain the intricacies of the Ruy Lopez, showing him the main lines. He is touched by it, but isn't committing himself in any way. He only looks at me without saying anything. I think that I am still a white boy, and therefore untrustworthy.

He is a subtle man, but obviously a deep thinker. He manipulates with his formidable size. His stare curdles the hardiest. Only his voice, on the side only, is pliantly soothing. I get inklings of what makes him who he is. What his *duty* is. I see the character in him, the way he deals with the malcontents, the victims. How he reacts to each of them. My doubts about understanding him when he rages, even to those he likes. He is multi-faceted. I hear stories about him: the bowling alley fights, over what or who, I need to know. He keeps everyone off balance until he drills them. Then he "shines." On the drill pad, he is in his element. There he gets respect from other sergeants. He creates in us a flow of movement, a syncopatic mastery stemming with this well-oiled strut. Like a conductor's baton, silently commanding a flow of grace.

I felt it in my limbs as they moved easily to a tempo he set. I was as much a choreographed dancer as a driller, my body gliding through the turns. "Hut, hut. Hut, two, three, four." Minutes later, only after he halted us did I notice another flight off to the side of the pad. Their thin sergeant, having the look of a martinet with his meticulous 505s, sparkling boots, and a thin mustache, swaggered toward us. He stopped when Huckaby eyeballed him. It was obvious that he wanted the drill pad and I sensed that he had just won the ground he covered and wasn't about to retreat. He brought his left arm up and peered at his watch. Now the tension was palpable. I could see other eyes on him. Seconds ticked by without response from Sgt. Hardin. The sun was bearing down on us, baking us as we rigidly awaited his command. I felt a droplet of sweat trickling down my face. Then I picked up the movement of the sergeant's right arm tapping the side of his leg, as if an imaginary swagger stick was there.

More seconds ticked by. Impatiently the sergeant spoke, "If you don't mind."

More seconds ticked by. The silence was endless.

Then Sgt. Hardin spoke lowly, "Be smart, now.

Flight, forward march.

With a crisp cadence, we moved like the machine we had become passed the grounded flight. We knew they were watching us. We were, after all, "the best."

WILLIAM POMEROY

ABOUT THE AUTHOR

William Pomeroy is a retired journalist and *Drillmaster* is his first published book. Pomeroy has won numerous writing awards including for his coverage of the shooting of President Ronald Reagan in 1981 in Washington DC.